THE SPOOK LIGHTS
AFFAIR

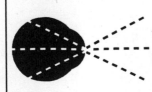

This Large Print Book carries the
Seal of Approval of N.A.V.H.

A CARPENTER AND QUINCANNON
MYSTERY

THE SPOOK LIGHTS
AFFAIR

MARCIA MULLER
BILL PRONZINI

THORNDIKE PRESS
A part of Gale, Cengage Learning

GALE
CENGAGE Learning®

Detroit • New York • San Francisco • New Haven, Conn • Waterville, Maine • London

Thorndike Press® Large Print Mystery.
The text of this Large Print edition is unabridged.
Other aspects of the book may vary from the original edition.
Set in 16 pt. Plantin.

LIBRARY OF CONGRESS CATALOGING-IN-PUBLICATION DATA

Muller, Marcia.
    The spook lights affair : a Carpenter and Quincannon mystery / by Marcia Muller, Bill Pronzini. — Large print edition.
        pages ; cm. — (Thorndike Press large print mystery)
        ISBN 978-1-4104-6434-7 (hardcover) — ISBN 1-4104-6434-2 (hardcover)
    1. Private investigators—California—San Francisco—Fiction. 2. Women detectives—California—San Francisco—Fiction. 3. San Francisco (Calif.)—History—19th century—Fiction. 4. Large type books. I. Pronzini, Bill. II. Title.
    PS3563.U397S66 2014
    813'.54—dc23   2013040082

Published in 2014 by arrangement with Tom Doherty Associate, LLC.

Printed in the United States of America
1 2 3 4 5 6 7 18 17 16 15 14

*For Mark Terry and Debbie Wilensky,
who live now where Carville-by-the-Sea
used to be*

1
SABINA

The main salon in the home atop San Francisco's Sutro Heights was ablaze with electric light from several ornate crystal chandeliers. Beyond the sheer white curtains at the row of French doors leading to the terrace and the raised overlook beyond, thickening swirls of a quickly encroaching fog were visible. The salon was the largest room in the relatively small, turreted residence Adolph Sutro had built around the cottage he'd purchased on these twenty-two clifftop acres in 1881, its dour design probably influenced by the architecture of his native Prussia. The salon's walls were pale yellow; the gowns of the "buds" — debutantes newly released into adult society — reflected all the hues of spring.

Sabina stood near the French doors, envying the buds' attire. Her own gown — a green crepe loaned to her by her society cousin, Callie French — seemed staid in comparison to the *peau de soies* and taffetas and chiffons and satins of the younger women. But she was here at the Sutro home on business, not to display her sense of fashion.

Young and older women and their escorts whirled around the polished floor to the music supplied by a five-piece orchestra. Adolph Sutro himself, "King of the Comstock Lode" and the city's new Populist Party mayor, sat in an ornately carved chair near the musicians, smiling benignly at his guests. With his bushy muttonchop whiskers and swooping mustache, his considerable girth and fine clothing, he resembled a monarch surveying his loyal subjects.

Sabina returned her gaze to the object of her surveillance: Virginia St. Ives, eighteen-year-old daughter of Joseph and Margaret St. Ives, prominent members of San Francisco society. Joseph St. Ives had made his fortune in the California gold fields, and like Adolph Sutro, had increased it substantially through shrewd real estate investments; his wife was related to the famous — some said infamous — Hearst family of mining and newspaper holdings. Virginia and her older brother, David, were heirs to an impressive fortune.

Unfortunately, at least as far as their

parents were concerned, both offspring refused to conform to their high station. David was reputedly one of the crowd of young blades who frequented the Cocktail Route, the nightly procession that began in the financial district as the banks and brokerage houses closed down, and ended, for some, in Uptown Tenderloin gambling parlors and bawdy houses and Barbary Coast dives. Virginia rejected the company of suitable young men, and had recently begun a misalliance with one Lucas Whiffing, a clerk in a downtown bicycle and sporting goods emporium. As if that weren't enough to make him an unsuitable suitor, Lucas presently lived with his family in Carville-by-the-Sea, a ragtag community mostly composed of abandoned streetcars that sprawled among the sand dunes some distance south of Sutro Heights.

Over the past two weeks, Virginia had been absent from the St. Ives' home twice, giving her parents flimsy and transparent excuses. A few days ago she had been seen dining in a public place with young Whiffing. Her parents were worried that Virginia's deepening involvement with him would lead to an elopement, or something even more tawdry; their fears had led them to engage Sabina the day before, to keep watch on their potentially wayward daughter while they went to Sacramento to attend a series of political functions important to Joseph's gubernatorial aspirations.

Sabina did not like the assignment — would, indeed, have refused it if John hadn't convinced her that it was an entrée to other lucrative jobs for members of San Francisco's upper class. She personally believed that a young woman had a right to pursue her passions, as she herself had done when she became a "Pink Rose" — one of the small, select group of female operatives of the Pinkerton International Detective Agency — at the tender age of twenty-two. Besides, she had researched the Whiffing family; Lucas might only be working as a store clerk, but he came of good stock. His father, James Whiffing, was a respectable and moderately well-off businessman. The fact that the Whiffings chose to live part of the year in Carville may have branded them as eccentric and offended the St. Ives' sensibilities, but Sabina saw nothing wrong with preferring bohemian beach life to city congestion.

Still, she had had to agree with John: Carpenter and Quincannon, Professional Detective Services, could scarcely afford to turn away well-heeled clients in these difficult economic times. The Panic of 1893 had been partially fueled by railroad overbuilding and the dubious financing thereof, which in turn culminated in bank failures and a steep decline in the value of the American dollar. Construction of new buildings and employment had fallen off, resulting in violent labor strikes. Businesses went under; agriculture was depressed by storm, drought, and — in the few good seasons — overproduction.

The situation, in this late spring of 1895, was less dire, but times remained hard for most of the populace. The wealthy, such as Adolph Sutro, remained solvent, of course, and continued to stage elaborate entertainments, such as the present one. The poor — such as the old woman named Annie who camped somewhere in Sabina's Russian Hill neighborhood and furtively ate the fish Sabina put out for her, mistaking it for cat food — were even more wretched than before.

It was people like the old woman who made Sabina somewhat contemptuous of Virginia St. Ives. She'd now spent an entire day, more or less, in constant company with the young blond-haired woman, and had found her petulant, selfish, and willful. The girl had barely spoken to her, except to attempt to issue orders as if she were a servant. ("Bring me my cup of tea. . . . Hand me that fan. . . . Help lace me up.")

Sabina was contemptuous of the young woman's parents as well: their insistence upon a "suitable" match for their daughter and their disregard for their son's irresponsible behavior grated upon her. Her own life had not been easy — her husband Stephen's sudden death from an assassin's bullet during a Pinkerton assignment in Denver five years ago had left her devastated — but she had learned to cope with its painful aspects and had built a new and rewarding life for herself here in San Francisco. Her partner had suffered his share of tragedy as well, having overcome a period of alcohol-soaked hell fueled by guilt over the accidental shooting death of a pregnant woman while an operative for the U.S. Secret Service, and reestablished himself as a splendid detective, an agreeable coworker, and a gentleman. Well, a gentleman most of the time. If only he would stop making amorous advances toward her . . .

Actually, though, John's advances were more worshipful, clumsy, and endearing than overtly seductive. He could be tough and dangerous when circumstances called for it; his vast ego was sometimes irritating, as was his tendency to bluster and grumble and seethe when things didn't go his way. But underneath he was a sensitive, easily wounded soul who read the poetry of Walt Whitman and Emily Dickinson for relaxation.

The musicians had switched from a series of lively rounds and reels to a Viennese waltz, and Virginia had reluctantly accepted an invitation to dance with her "escort" for the evening, her sleekly handsome, sandy-haired older brother. The girl looked beautiful in her flowing white gown, a pink silk scarf adorned with butterflies fluttering from her swanlike neck, a small crocheted chatelaine handbag on her wrist. Sabina moved her feet and swayed a little, remembering when she and Stephen had stepped on to the dance floors in various ballrooms in Chicago and Denver. She hadn't danced in years, not since his death. Would she ever again?

Not with anyone in this crowd. For one thing, she was working. And for another, none of the dozen or so men of all ages who had approached her had appealed to her in the slightest.

She almost wished John were here. He had offered to accompany her — she could easily have gotten him an invitation — and he would have made a handsome escort, but he lacked the patience and prudence for this kind of elaborate affair. It would have bored him silly, perhaps to the point of saying or doing something rash. And his presence might well have been a distraction: she would have had to keep an eye on him as well as on Virginia. Besides, he had more important business on his mind — such as the recent Wells, Fargo Express robbery and his hope for word from one of his Barbary Coast contacts that would put him on the trail of the holdup artist and the substantial reward the company was offering.

Sabina sighed and moved to a slightly different vantage point. Among the guests she spied Ralstons and Crockers, Huntingtons and Judahs. Many of San Francisco's social elite were present, as an invitation from Adolph Sutro was considered as something of a command performance. It was such an exclusive Friday evening gathering that not even Callie and her husband, Hugh, the president of the Miners Bank, had been invited.

Callie had nonetheless graciously instructed Sabina in comportment and how to remain inconspicuous at such events. "Take up a position against a wall away from the seated ladies and the refreshment buffet. Appear to be having a good time, but don't allow your gaze to linger on anyone too long. Loop a fan around your wrist and when you're asked to dance, flutter it and say you're feeling a bit faint. If any of the gentlemen persist, fix them with one of your icy stares."

"I do not have an icy stare!"

Callie had snorted in a most unladylike fashion. "Now," she'd continued, "and this is important: do not fidget, do not consult any timepiece, smile at and nod to any and all who acknowledge you, and pay no attention to any of those hippopotamus-faced matrons who give you pitying glances because they consider you a wallflower."

Dear Callie. Sabina had followed her advice to the letter and it had gotten her through the evening well enough thus far. But she was glad she hadn't taken another piece of advice her cousin had dispensed, that she would look even better in her gown if she were to wear one of Callie's Invigorator Corsets. "Doctor recommended to smooth your shape while not unduly compressing your organs. And they support your back and shoulders, so as to expand your chest."

"No, no, no!" Sabina had exclaimed. "The last thing I want or need is to have my chest expanded. These gowns are bad enough: I could trip over those flounces and the lace makes my neck itch. I can put up with that for an evening, but I draw the line at a corset."

The orchestra was now playing another, even more spirited tune. One of Charles Crocker's heirs clasped to his considerable corporation a young woman whose expression said she wished someone would rescue her. Another of the buds grimaced in pain as a member of Mark Hopkins's family stepped on her foot. Old gentlemen ogled buds and matrons alike; most of those who noticed sniffed with disdain. A few, however, condescended to take the floor with those who asked them, and seemed to be thoroughly enjoying themselves.

Virginia St. Ives was not one of them.

The rebellious debutante and her brother had left the dance floor; now they were standing near the buffet, David partaking of the generous feast, while Virginia conferred with a singularly unattractive young woman named Grace DeBrett. Grace was evidently Virginia's best friend and had visited her that afternoon to squeal over her gown and accessories. When their present conversation ended, Grace shrugged and moved away to the buffet. Virginia turned, saw Sabina watching her; a frown darkened her pretty features and she stared back for several seconds, then flounced around the dance floor to Sabina's side. Anger blazed in the girl's blue eyes.

"Look, you," she said in a harsh, low tone, grabbing Sabina's forearm, "must you watch me every single minute?"

Sabina removed her hand and responded quietly and courteously, even though she would have preferred to shake or slap some manners into the post-deb. "You know that's what your parents hired me to do."

"Well, it's gone on long enough! I can't go anywhere or do anything without your eyes all over me. You haven't the right to even be at this party, you . . . you common old chaperone!"

The words smarted, mainly because Sabina *did* feel a bit like an old chaperone in her borrowed gown. She swallowed a sharp retort, answered in the same even tones, "Such displays of temper are not becoming, young lady. You should learn to respect your elders."

The bud's mouth tightened. "I see no reason to respect anyone who keeps harassing me."

"You're not being harassed, Miss St. Ives. Merely looked after for your own good, as

17

per your father's wishes."

"My father's wishes! I haven't seen or communicated with Lucas Whiffing in . . . I don't even remember the last time."

"You had a rendezvous with him only a few days ago. That and your two poorly explained absences in the past two weeks are the reasons I was employed."

"Well . . . what if I did see him just once? A *public* rendezvous at a respectable restaurant. What's wrong with that?"

"You know how your parents feel about Mr. Whiffing —"

"I don't care how they feel!" Her voice had risen; a couple nearby turned to look at her. "They don't trust me. They think I'll toss my bonnet over the windmill if I haven't already!"

Sabina was surprised. Of course Virginia would know the euphemism for having premarital relations — all young women of whatever station did — but for her to speak the words in such surroundings as these, and within hearing of others . . .

The post-deb's eyes were welling with tears. She put a hand to her brow and said in a loud, dramatic voice, "Now see what you've done? You've made me cry!"

"Hush. People are staring."

"Let them stare. I don't care, I don't care

about *anything* anymore! You'll see! You and my parents and everybody else!" And with that she whirled and rushed away.

Several of the guests cast disapproving looks at Sabina, who ignored them as she set out after the girl. But the swirl of dancers impeded her progress; Virginia had passed through the door from the salon into the front part of the house before she could catch her.

The hallway beyond the door was deserted. The ladies' room was close by and Sabina thought the deb must have gone in there. But when she quickly checked, there was no sign of Virginia inside. From there Sabina hastened into the front vestibule — just in time to see her charge moving toward the main entrance doors.

"Virginia!"

The girl gave no indication that she'd heard. She yanked one of the doors open and plunged through into the torchlit darkness beyond.

Sabina ran to the door and stopped it from closing, but not before an edge of it caught the hem of her cumbersome skirt. She pulled free, tearing the fabric, and looked out. Through the cold, billowing fog that swirled across the grounds, she spied Virginia hurrying at an angle away from the main carriageway where the row of parked coaches that had brought the guests waited.

Hurrying where? And why had the silly girl fled without taking either wrap or coat?

2
SABINA

The house's heavy front door banged shut behind her as she stepped outside. Virginia St. Ives was not quite running through the side gardens toward a tree-bordered pathway that branched off toward the sea, her white skirts drawn up at the waist and billowing around her slender legs. She glanced back once, then cast her eyes to the uneven ground ahead of her and kept them there.

Sabina had no choice but to follow. The night's chill penetrated the thin fabric of her gown, started her shivering. The girl must be mad to have come out here dressed as she was. Yes, and she herself must be mad as well to be pursuing her in the same coatless state. But there was no turning back now, not until she found out where Virginia was bound in such a hurry. Some sort of rendezvous with Lucas Whiffing, possibly, but why hadn't she taken the time to bundle up before leaving the house?

Fog-laden wind rushed at Sabina as she crossed the front terrace, and one of her hairpins was blown loose and brushed her cheek as it was flung away. Brine and eucalyptus scents filled her nostrils. In the distance she could hear the roar of the sea as it crashed on the rocks below the Cliff House construction site.

Groves of trees — mainly wind-sculpted cypress interspersed with eucalyptus and palms — covered the vast property. The gardens and other open spaces were dotted with statuary. She dodged past one of the statues, a Greek goddess with stone tresses and draped gown like a figure frozen in time. Adolph Sutro was said to have a fascination with these lifeless creations; in addition to mythological figures, two huge stone lions stood beside the arched gate to the grounds and the main carriageway was lined with stags, does, fawns, and other wild creatures. Sabina didn't understand it. To her, such statues were cold as the grave, particularly on nights like this. Memento mori — reminders of the fate that awaits all.

The grounds were lit by flickering torches that had been spaced at intervals along the carriageway and close to the large fountain in its center loop; others illuminated some of the larger statues. Servants must have filled the torches with kerosene for the party, for their flames flickered high — yellow, orange, blue, green. Their light created an eerie, glowing effect on the tendrils of mist that swirled among the trees, and allowed Sabina to keep Virginia in sight as she gave chase. The young ninny was now almost into the shadows cast by the copse of eucalyptus.

Someone called out — one of the coach drivers, three of whom were standing together at the edge of the carriageway. Neither Virginia nor Sabina paid any attention to the call. The damp, uneven ground caused Sabina to slip and stumble, once to nearly lose her balance. She considered kicking off her — Callie's — little formal slippers, but that would do more harm than good. Running in her stockings might make her footing more sure, but it would also send fresh chills and shivers through her body and allow wind-strewn eucalyptus pods and pine cones to bite into the soles of her feet. Barely in time, she saw and side-stepped a gopher hole. Even Adolph Sutro's gardeners couldn't defeat the ubiquitous California gophers.

Ahead, Virginia cast another look over her shoulder just before vanishing among the eucalyptus, but she was out of sight only for as long as it took Sabina to reach the trees. Then she saw the girl on the cinder pathway, passing a fog-draped structure she recognized as the gazebo with peaked roof, ornate posts, and fancywork that Sutro had reportedly imported from France. Virginia's destination now seemed clear: the broad, semicircular sea-view overlook that rose high behind the house, on which summer parties were held and which contained a water tower, observation platform, and enclosed photograph gallery. Where Lucas Whiffing waited? There didn't seem to be any other reason why the girl would have taken such a circuitous route to the overlook, instead of going there directly across the rear terrace.

The fog was thicker here, great moist coils of it that obscured the treetops and the upper edges of the parapet, and the distant pounding of the sea louder. The Potato Patch foghorn off Point Lobos bellowed mournfully. The hard cinders bit into Sabina's chilled feet; the slippers and her stockings were no doubt damaged beyond repair. Callie's gown, too, probably. She was so cold and wet now that a fear of pneumonia tugged at her mind. The fear made her furious. When she caught up with Miss St. Ives, she'd give the girl a tongue-lashing she'd never forget.

Virginia had reached and started up the seaward stairs to the overlook. Sabina called out for her to stop and wait, but the shouted words had no effect; typically defiant, the girl didn't seem to care that she was being pursued. She ran up the steps two at a time, a wraithlike figure in the sinuous vapor. By the time Sabina reached the foot of the stairs, her charge had vanished onto the flagstone floor above.

Sabina made the climb as quickly as she was able, enduring little shoots of pain at every step. When she reached the top, she could see no sign of Virginia in the thick gray swirls. She paused with ears straining, heard the faint slap of the girl's hurrying steps. Moments later those sounds ceased and others took their place — scramblings and scrapings that Sabina couldn't identify.

She moved ahead cautiously, swiping her hands through the fog in an effort to clear it so she could determine where Virginia had gone. After a few steps, a vague, ghost-like luminosity appeared ahead to her left — the deb's white gown. The figure seemed poised a couple of feet above floor level, as if Virginia had climbed up onto the parapet at the overlook's outer edge. But surely she wouldn't have done anything that foolish —

Yes, she would. And had. The fog curls parted just enough ahead to reveal the spectral shape of the girl some thirty yards distant, standing between two of the statues mounted on the parapet, facing toward the sea with her arms bent away from her body. She was alone atop the wall; if anyone else lurked nearby, he was hidden by the mist.

What was she doing up there? The stones were slippery, dangerous in the wind and fog; beyond and beneath the wall was a mostly sheer drop of several hundred feet to the Great Highway.

"Virginia!"

The fog muffled Sabina's cry, and she shouted again. To no avail. Virginia continued to stand, wavering slightly from side to side now, her gown making an audible fluttery sound —

And then, to Sabina's horrified amazement, the girl flung herself forward and disappeared.

There was a shriek, shrill and long-drawn, then thudding, sliding sounds that carried above the voice of the wind — the sounds of a body tumbling down the cliffside.

It took Sabina several seconds to stumble ahead to the parapet. Just as she reached it, her foot struck something lying on the

26

flagstones. She ignored it for the moment, leaning over the wall between the two statues to peer downward. What she saw brought another shiver that had nothing to do with the cold. A strip of ground some eight feet wide stretched out beneath, the only section of it visible straight ahead where it sloped down to the cliff edge. That part was thinly covered with purple-flowered ice plant, mashed down where Virginia's body had landed and slid through. Beyond the ice plant, the cliff fell away in a sheer vertical drop.

Sabina drew back, and again her foot brushed against the object on the stones. She bent to pick it up, saw that it was the chatelaine handbag Virginia had carried. Clutching it, she glanced to her left. A winding set of steps chiseled into the bare rock led down to the highway below, she remembered, but the hovering grayness hid their exact location. They weren't an option in any case. The stone steps would be slick and slippery and the descent treacherous; it would be folly to risk climbing down them in the darkness, even if there were a chance of finding the girl alive at the bottom. And she didn't see how there could be. It was virtually impossible for anyone to have survived such a long fall.

Why had the mad little fool done this to herself?

Why?

Badly shaken, Sabina took the direct route back to the mansion, down the staircase at the opposite end of the overlook. Fog-laced shadows hid her from the guests behind the lighted ballroom windows as she hurried along the rim of the lower terrace. She made her way to the servant's entrance, found the door there unlocked. Her sudden entrance and her disheveled appearance brought shocked stares from three members of the kitchen staff.

"There's been a terrible accident," she told them. "One of you fetch Mr. Sutro. Quickly!"

Her voice sounded as benumbed as her body felt, but the note of command in it was still strong enough to brook no argument. The male member of the staff nodded and hurried out. One of the two women guided Sabina over near the cookstove, where its pulsing heat soon warmed her blood and sent pins and needles tingling through her chilled flesh.

She realized then that she still held Virginia's handbag. Impulse led her to unsnap the clasp and reach inside. The usual feminine

28

necessities, and a folded sheet of notepaper that Sabina drew out. She knew what it was even before she spread it open and read the lines written on it in a firm, girlish hand.

I cannot bear to go on living in misery, facing a hopeless future. Everyone will be better off without me. Good-bye.

Virginia

So young, and so foolish!

Portly and bewhiskered Adolph Sutro appeared just then, with a second, liveried servant in tow. Sabina had been introduced to the mayor briefly when she arrived and he remembered her, though he'd had no idea of her profession until she revealed it as part of her terse explanation of what had happened. As taken aback as he was by her words, and by those in the suicide note she handed him, he wasted no time with frivolous questions but took immediate charge.

He sent the liveried servant to quietly summon David St. Ives and a doctor Sabina didn't know named Bowers to the front terrace. "Tell them only that there is an emergency," he said. "And bring along a brace of hand lanterns." Then he instructed one of the kitchen women to fetch Sabina's beaver coat, which she described, and the

29

other to find shoes to replace the ruined slippers. In less than five minutes she was bundled and reshod and almost warm again, only to have Sutro lead her back out into the cold darkness and around to the front where Virginia's brother and Dr. Bowers waited.

David St. Ives was grimly incredulous at the news of his sister's plunge. As Sabina and the three men hurriedly settled into the coach that belonged to the St. Ives family, he said, "Suicide? Virginia? I don't believe it."

"The note *is* in her handwriting?" Sabina said.

"Yes, it's hers. 'Living in misery . . . hopeless future . . . everyone will be better off without me.' None of that makes any sense. She had everything to live for."

"Obviously she didn't think so. Young girls take life very seriously, Mr. St. Ives. And love as well."

"Love? She wasn't in love with anyone."

"Your father believed she might be."

"That damned rascal Lucas Whiffing? Nonsense. She was upset at not being allowed to see him, but not despondent over it."

"Isn't it possible she simply slipped and fell?" Mayor Sutro asked Sabina.

"No, sir. She jumped from the parapet."

"You saw this clearly? Fog has a way of distorting what one observes from a distance."

"Clearly enough not to be mistaken."

"I still don't believe it." David St. Ives was glaring at her; she could feel as well as see the intensity of his stare in the lantern light as the coach rattled at a rapid pace along the carriageway. He was an arrogant, vain young man whom Sabina had disliked on their first meeting; his attitude now was even more overbearing and offensive, despite his obvious grief. "You were hired to watch over my sister, Mrs. Carpenter," he said angrily. "How could you let something like this happen?"

"I had no way of knowing what she was planning to do. I thought she was intent on meeting someone on the parapet. Lucas Whiffing, perhaps."

"Did you speak to her when you saw she was alone out there? Try to save her?"

"There was no time to do either. I called her name, but either she didn't hear me or ignored my shout —"

"I still hold you responsible. You had words with her in the salon before she ran out. Everyone heard what was said."

"Her voice was raised, yes, but not mine.

I said nothing to provoke her. Besides, she'd already made up her mind — the suicide note had already been written."

"Damn the suicide note! You could have saved her and you didn't — that's the inexcusable fact. You'll pay dearly for your dereliction, I promise you that!"

Mayor Sutro, sitting on the seat facing David St. Ives, leaned across to grip his knee. "That's enough, young man. This is tragedy enough without you compounding it with threats."

St. Ives muttered something under his breath, then lapsed into a brooding silence.

They were passing through the estate's arched entrance now, onto Point Lobos Avenue. The coach driver whipped his brace of horses into a fast downhill run. The fog was so dense that the Cliff House and Sutro Baths, the mayor's new and as yet unfinished gifts to the city, were invisible along the promontories below. And the intersection with the Great Highway materialized so abruptly that the driver was forced to brake sharply in order to make the turn.

No lights showed along the highway's sand-strewn expanse. There was little traffic in this part of the city at night, especially when the ocean fog was this thick. The coach clattered ahead, its side lanterns illuminating the bottom edges of the bare cliff wall. Abruptly, then, the driver braked again and the rig ground to a rocking halt. Sabina thought it must be because he had seen Virginia St. Ives' broken remains in the roadway ahead. But when she alighted along with the three men, Sutro and St. Ives carrying the lanterns, she saw that this was not the case.

What lay on the highway, in close to the cliff, was a rock the size of a small boulder that had evidently been dislodged during the fall. The girl's body must be somewhere close by, hidden by the restless mist. But to Sabina's surprise and consternation, this, too, turned out not to be the case.

A long, careful search of the highway revealed no sign of Virginia, alive or dead.

"It's possible someone came along and found her," Mayor Sutro said when the four of them stood with the driver in a bewildered group alongside the coach. "But my home is the nearest habitation and we would surely have encountered anyone entering the grounds. Nor did we pass another vehicle on the way down Point Lobos."

"Dickey's Road House is less than a mile from here," Sabina said.

"Yes, that's so. Unlikely, but . . . we'll drive

down there and see."

"If she wasn't taken to Dickey's," David St. Ives said, "then she *couldn't* have gone over the cliff. She must be caught on a tree or outcropping somewhere up above. Unconscious, or we'd have heard her cry for help."

Sabina would have liked to believe that, but she didn't. "The strip of ground below the parapet was empty," she said, "and marks in the ice plant are visible to the edge."

"Then she must have fallen all the way down," Mayor Sutro said. "The cliff face is sheer below that strip."

Dr. Bowers spoke for the first time. "I'm afraid there's no doubt of it, if this belongs to the girl. I found it near the dislodged rock."

What he was holding in his hand, outstretched into the glow of the mayor's lantern, was a wisp of white cloth caught on a torn-off cypress limb. Sabina recognized it immediately: the distinctive butterfly scarf that had fluttered from the post-deb's neck as she'd danced in the salon.

"It's Virginia's," her brother confirmed.

The round trip to Dickey's Road House, a popular breakfast stop for some of the more hardy and adventurous habitués of

34

the Cocktail Route, took half an hour. And proved futile. No one there knew anything about Virginia St. Ives.

On the solemn ride back to Sutro Heights, David broke a long silence by putting voice to what Sabina and the others were thinking. "If nobody came by and found her . . . my God, then what happened to her body?"

3
QUINCANNON

The note, just delivered by runner to Quincannon's Leavenworth Street flat, was printed in Ezra Bluefield's distinctive backslanted hand and typically brief and to the point:

> *Bob Cantwell, 209 Spear Street #3. Information for sale Express matter. Tell him C. Riley sent you.*
>
> *E.B.*

A smile pleated Quincannon's thick freebooter's beard. Leave it to Bluefield to ferret out a lead no one else had yet discovered. Saving the life of the owner of the Scarlet Lady saloon, one of the less odious Barbary Coast deadfalls, and then cultivating the ex-miner's friendship had been repaid many times over. Bluefield had his pudgy fingers on the pulse of the city's criminal activities in and out of the Coast and there was little he didn't know or couldn't find out through his extensive contacts.

The Express matter referred to a daring robbery by a lone masked man of the Wells, Fargo Express office one week ago, in which nearly $35,000 in greenbacks — a special company shipment that had just come in from the south by railroad — had been taken. The company's detectives and the city's bluecoats had failed to turn up a single lead, not surprisingly in the latter case given the general incompetence of the police.

In such cases as this, when all else failed, Wells, Fargo had been known to pay a reward of ten percent to private agencies such as Carpenter and Quincannon, Professional Detective Services, for the return of the stolen cash and the arrest and conviction of the thief. Thirty-five hundred dollars was a considerable lure and Quincannon had undertaken his own investigation in pursuit of it. Thus far he had made as little headway as the other investigators, but if Bluefield's tip panned out, he would lay claim to the reward and add another triumph to an already auspicious career.

Bob Cantwell, eh? Quincannon, whose memory was both photographic and encyclopedic, knew the names of most of the city's snitches and information sellers, as well as those of scores of grifters, yeggs, confidence tricksters, and other criminals, but Cantwell's was not among them. Yet the lad must be on the shady side if he possessed knowledge of the Wells, Fargo Express robbery. A gambler, professional or amateur? Charles Riley was the hardshell owner of the House of Chance, one of the Uptown Tenderloin sporting palaces.

Before Bluefield's runner had brought the sealed envelope, Quincannon had resigned himself to a lonely evening in his rooms, reading from Wordsworth's *Poems, in Two Volumes.* Usually both solitude and poetry relaxed him; on this evening, however, neither helped ease a brooding restlessness. His mind kept straying to Sabina's presence at one of Adolph Sutro's lavish parties. Unescorted presence, blast it, in the midst of what was sure to be a gaggle of predatory males, accompanied and unaccompanied, who considered a comely widow fair game. Why the devil had she refused to allow him to join her tonight? True, she was on a job, a rather dull one with no real need of his company, but that had nothing to do with her refusal. "I'll be busy, John, and you know you dislike formal gatherings among the social elite." Social elite. Bah! Hobnobbing with highbrows may have been one of his least favorite activities, but where his partner was concerned, he was willing to put up with anything in order to forestall a potential assault on her favors.

Well, he would just have to trust to Sabina's avowed distinterest in the attentions of the male sex in general, and to his conviction that if anyone succeeded in breaking through her defenses, that someone would be John Quincannon. Now that he had a lead to the Wells, Fargo reward, he would be too busy himself for any more brooding. Money honestly earned and the thrill of the chase were even stronger motivations than his pursuit of Sabina, and $3,500 was the kind of prize that stirred his blood to a fine simmer.

He shut off the gas heater, strapped on his Navy Colt, plucked his greatcoat from the hall tree, and hurried out into the cold foggy night in search of a cab.

The section of Spear Street where Bob Cantwell resided was close to the Embarcadero and the massive bulk of the Ferry Building. Flanking its dark length was a mix of warehouses, stores operated by ship's chandlers and outfitters, cheap saloons, and lodging houses that catered to seamen, laborers, and shop workers. Whoever

Cantwell was, he was none too well off to call this district home.

Quincannon stepped out of the hack on the corner of Spear and Mission streets. There was no one abroad as he started down Spear, at least no one visible to him in the swirling gray mist that blanketed the area. He walked swiftly and watchfully nonetheless, one hand inside his coat resting on the holstered Navy. Muggings were not so common here as in the Barbary Coast, north of Market, but the waterfront was still a rough place on dark nights; a man alone, particularly a man who was rather well dressed, was fair prey for footpads. Out on the Bay foghorns moaned in ceaseless rhythm. As he crossed Howard he had glimpses of pier sheds and the masts and steam funnels of anchored ships, gray-black and indistinct like disembodied ghosts.

Number 209 took shape ahead — a three-story firetrap built of warping wood, unpainted and sorely in need of carpentry work, set between another, smaller lodging house and a rope-and-twine chandler's. Smears of electric light showed at the front entrance, illuminating a painted sign that grew readable as he neared: DRAKE'S REST — ROOMS BY DAY, WEEK, MONTH.

Inside he found a short hallway, a set of

stairs, and a small common room, all of which smelled of salt-damp and decay. In the common room, a scrawny harridan stood feeding crackers to an equally scrawny parrot in a wire cage. It was even money as to which owned the more evil eye, the woman or the bird. Her watery gaze ran Quincannon up and down in a hungry fashion, as if she would have liked nothing better than to knock him on the head and relieve him of his valuables.

The hunger, he soon discovered, was because she was the owner of the lodging house and there was a vacant room that wanted filling. Her interest in him waned when he informed her that he was there to see one of her tenants, Bob Cantwell, on a business matter.

"What business would a swell like you have with the likes of Bob Cantwell?" she asked.

"Mine and his, madam."

"Madam," she said. "Hah! Number three, upstairs, but he's not in. Seldom is, nights."

"Do you know where I can find him?"

"No. How would I know?" But the gleam in her eye said otherwise. She was another of the breed, Quincannon thought sourly, who gave out little or no information free of charge.

41

He fished in his pocket for coins. Faugh. He had only two, both silver dollars. Reluctantly he removed one, flipped it high so that it caught the light from a pair of lamps. The woman's greedy gaze followed the coin's path up and back down into his palm. She licked her thin lips.

"Now then," he said. "Where does Bob spend his evenings?"

"I don't keep track of my lodgers."

The devil she didn't. He flipped the coin again. "Frequents the Tenderloin, doesn't he?"

"So I've heard. Among other sinful places."

"Such as the Barbary Coast?"

"The devil's playground," she said, and the parrot cackled as if in agreement.

"A gambling man, is he?"

"Aye, and what man isn't?"

"What's his business, that he can afford such a pastime?"

"Real estate salesman, so he claims."

"Which firm?"

"Hammond Realtors, Battery Street. But you won't find him there this time of night. Off carousing and playing devil's dice, or drinking in some saloon if he can't afford worse."

"Dice is his preferred game, is it?"

"So I hear tell. More'n once he's lost his wages and been late with his rent. Next time he'll be out on the street."

That explained the connection between Cantwell and Charles Riley. Dice games, craps, and chuck-a-luck were the House of Chance's specialties. Cantwell must have approached Riley with an offer to sell him his information in exchange for cash or gambling chits, and been turned down; Riley's only business interest was in relieving his customers, more or less legitimately, of their hard-earned dollars.

"Where does Bob do his drinking in this area when he's shy of funds?" Quincannon asked. "Any saloon in particular?"

The crone's eyes were still on the silver dollar. Its shine and her greed kept her from any more pretense. "The Bucket of Beer," she said.

"And where would that be?"

"Clay Street, near the Embarcadero."

"Any others?"

"None as I know of."

Quincannon tossed her the silver dollar. She caught it expertly, bit it between snaggle teeth. The parrot cackled and said, "Ho, money! Ho, money!" She glared at the bird, then cursed it as Quincannon turned for the door. She seemed genuinely concerned that the parrot might break out of its cage and take the coin away from her.

The Bucket of Beer Saloon was a typical waterfront watering hole tucked in among the dingy warehouses strung along lower Clay Street — smoky and poorly lighted, decorated with seafaring impedimenta and redolent of beer, tobacco, and close-packed humanity. The usual sifting of sawdust shared the floor with a rank of none-too-clean spittoons. There were less than a dozen customers on this night, most of them bellied up to the long bar — all male except for a plump and painted soiled dove trolling for a customer and having no luck. She spied Quincannon as he entered, sidled over to him.

"Foul night, ain't it, dearie?" she asked hopefully.

"It is that."

"Kind of night it takes more than liquor to warm a man's cockles."

Quincannon allowed as how his were warm enough as they stood.

"Pity. You're a fine-looking gent, you are, just the sort little Molly likes."

At a guess, "little" Molly weighed in the neighborhood of a hundred and fifty pounds. "Some other time," he lied. "I'm here on business tonight, with a lad named Bob Cantwell. Know him, Molly?"

Her rouged mouth pinched into a lemony pucker. "Know him and wish I didn't. Cheapskate. Won't never even offer to quench a lady's thirst."

"Is he here now?"

"Oh, he's here. Don't know him, eh? Buy a lady a whiskey to keep off the chill if I point him out?"

The only coin Quincannon had in his pocket was the second silver dollar. His thrifty Scot's nature rebelled at yet another overly generous outlay, but he pressed the coin into Molly's moist palm anyway; a prostitute was as deserving of his largesse as the crone at 209 Spear, if not more so. Her eyes widened and she favored him with a crooked-toothed smile and an effusive, "Oh, what a gent you are, sir!" After which she aimed a pudgy arm at a man seated alone at a table next to a glowing potbellied stove. "That's him, Bob Cantwell," she said, and hurried off to the bar.

Bob Cantwell was a scrawny individual in his early twenties, the owner of sparse sandy hair and a skimpy mustache to match. He sat slump-shouldered inside a heavy corduroy coat, staring morosely into a tankard of grog — the look and posture of a man

45

drowning his sorrows. The empty chair opposite the real estate salesman scraped as Quincannon pulled it out far enough to accommodate his bulk.

Cantwell cast a startled look at him across the table. "Here, what's the idea? I don't want company —"

"Bob Cantwell?"

"What if I am? Who're you?"

"My name is of no consequence to you. My business is."

"What kind of business?" Cantwell asked warily.

"Not the police kind. You've no worries there, Bob."

"Well, then? What do you want?"

Quincannon said, "Charles Riley tells me you have information regarding the Wells, Fargo Express matter."

The sudden change in Cantwell's demeanor was little short of miraculous. The undernourished frame jerked upright, the sandy mustache bristled, the pale blue eyes glittered with sudden avarice. One hand reached across the table as if to pluck at Quincannon's coat sleeve, stopping just short of its mark.

"And if I do?" he said in a lowered voice. "It doesn't come free."

"Little does in this world. What is it

you know?"

"Plenty. Plenty. How much will you pay?"

"That depends on the information. How much do you think it's worth?"

Cantwell leaned forward, the pale eyes taking in the expensive cut of Quincannon's greatcoat and custom-made derby. While he was scrutinizing, his other hand plucked items from his pocket that made audible clicking sounds. There was no hint of moroseness left in him now; he fairly quivered with greed. It had been financial sorrows he'd been drowning in his grog: a lack of sufficient funds to indulge his gambling vice, no doubt. The clicking of the pair of dice in his hand had what might be described as an eager sound.

"Two hundred dollars," he said. "Cash on the barrelhead."

Quincannon shoved back his chair, got to his feet, and started to turn away.

"Wait! Wait! What I know is worth that much. Every cent of it."

"Yes? What do you know?"

"The name of the holdup man."

"That's not worth two hundred."

"And where you can find him and the money. That *is.*"

Quincannon sat down again. "I'll pay half your asking price."

47

"No. Two hundred or nothing —"

"Nothing, then." He stood back up.

Cantwell said quickly, "You're not the only one interested. Somebody else will pay two hundred."

"Charles Riley wouldn't pay it. No one else will, either, or you and I wouldn't be having this conversation."

The dice clicks grew agitated. Anxiety visibly leavened the lad's greed; he could see his much-coveted cash windfall slipping away. "All right, sir," he said. "All right. I'll settle for one hundred."

Quincannon reoccupied the chair, hitching it around toward Cantwell — to get closer to the warmth from the stove, but the youngster thought otherwise. He scooted his chair away the same distance, as if he were afraid of an attack. Cantwell was a coward, among his other shortcomings. Quincannon grinned at him, a fierce grin that was half wolf, half dragon. He took his time loading and lighting his stubby briar, then removed a greenback from his billfold and flattened his palm over it on the table, leaving a portion free so that Cantwell could make out the denomination.

"Say! That's only twenty dollars."

"The rest when you've told me what you know."

"How do I know you'll pay me?"

"You'll get nothing if you don't talk. Except maybe a cuffed ear."

Cantwell swallowed, took a quick drink of grog, and swallowed that. "You won't tell anyone the word came from me?"

"Not if what you tell me is the truth."

"It will be. I swear it." After a furtive glance around, even though no one in the smoky room was within listening distance, Cantwell leaned forward and again spoke in an undertone. "Jack Travers."

The name was unfamiliar to Quincannon. "Local?"

"No. From Los Angeles."

"How do you know him? As a confederate?"

"No! I'm not a crook, I'm a respectable citizen."

Claptrap, Quincannon thought. "Then how do you know him?"

Cantwell hesitated. Then, "Jack Travers is my cousin."

"And how do you know he's the Express bandit?"

"He . . . bragged to me about it. A holdup that would put him in clover for the rest of his life."

"But not specifically the Wells, Fargo job, eh?"

"No. But it couldn't be anything else. Jack was too excited, and there has been no other large robbery recently. Besides . . . he's been in trouble with the law before. He spent a few years in prison for armed robbery."

"When did he do his bragging? Before or after the deed?"

"Before," Cantwell said. "A week before. He came to my lodgings one night. I hadn't seen him in years, since I moved to San Francisco, but he knew that I work for a real estate firm. He demanded I fix him up with a place where he could . . . hole up for a while."

"And you did his bidding for a price."

"No, sir. He threatened me into it." Cantwell's mouth quirked bitterly. "Jack's half again my size and a damned bully. He . . . well, he used to beat on me when we were kids."

That explained why Cantwell was willing to sell out his cousin. Money the primary reason, revenge the secondary. The little poltroon was too cowardly and too afraid of Jack Travers to try cutting himself in for a percentage of the stolen loot, yet too hungry for cash to feed his gambling habit to have turned Travers in to the coppers. A contemptible Judas whose price had been halved to one hundred pieces of silver.

"Where's the hideout, Bob?"

"Why do you want to know? If you're not a policeman, what are you? A Wells, Fargo detective?"

"My business is none of yours."

"But you are planning to arrest him?"

"Likewise none of your concern. Answer the question."

Cantwell gave his lips a nervous licking. "You won't tell him I told you? You won't say anything about talking to me?"

"Nary a word. Now where can I find him?"

"A cottage on Telegraph Hill. Drifter's Alley, off Filbert below Pioneer Park. The alley's a cul-de-sac, with just two cottages and a vacant lot between. He's in the second."

Quincannon knew the approximate location. He nodded, and then asked, "Have you been to see your cousin since the robbery?"

"Why would I? I want nothing more to do with him. He can rot in jail or in hell for all I care."

"Then how do you know he's still in the cottage?"

"He must be. Jack said he'd need the place for some time, to let things cool down, as he put it. And he hasn't returned the key."

Quincannon considered. Hearsay and

51

speculation — a thin brew for one hundred dollars. On the other hand, he had no better lead and there was enough tantalizing circumstantial evidence in Bob Cantwell's story to make it worth following up.

He took his hand off the twenty-dollar greenback. Cantwell snatched it up instantly and made it disappear. The dice in his other hand rattled greedily as Quincannon removed four more twenties from his billfold, folded the notes, passed them over. How long Cantwell remained in possession of his newfound wealth depended on the whims of Lady Luck: he would be in a dice game within minutes of their parting. Which was immediate, Quincannon having nothing more to say to the little weasel. For the nonce, anyway.

He was now out a considerable amount of cash — one hundred and two dollars, to be exact — and his night's work had only just begun. If it developed that Jack Travers was not the Wells, Fargo Express bandit, the money he had just handed over would eventually be recovered even if he had to take it out of Bob Cantwell's hide a dollar at a time.

4
QUINCANNON

Only the western slopes of Telegraph Hill were habitable; the hill fell away so steeply to the east that there were no streets leading up, just foot trails and a scattered few wooden stairways. Although it was much the more difficult route, Quincannon chose the eastern ascent because it was not far from the Bucket of Beer and because a cab ride around to and up Dupont Street, the hill's main thoroughfare, would have taken twice as long as an uphill climb on foot.

The fog had thinned somewhat along the Embarcadero and on the lower section of Broadway, but it closed in around him like cotton batting as he hiked up the long wooden stairway from Montgomery Street. It was a potentially treacherous climb at night in weather such as this, there being no streetlights above Montgomery and the steps, more than two hundred of them, being wet and slippery; he clung to the railing with his left hand, his right perched on the butt of his Navy. But he met no one on the stairs, no one on the footpaths above. He knew the area well enough, and a good thing else he might have gotten lost in the misty tangle leading up to Pioneer Park.

When he reached the hill's summit, he was barely winded. He might have been nearing his fortieth year, but he kept himself in prime physical condition through regular wanderings around the city by shank's mare. Nor was he much aware of the night's chill and damp. Nothing warmed his blood like the prospect of a confrontation with lawbreakers, the more so when a substantial reward was at stake. Like his detective father before him, John Quincannon thrived on the hunt.

The fog was so thick here he could barely make out the tall signal-pole from which the city's time ball fell each noon to tell mariners and residents that the sun was crossing the meridian. It took him a little time to find his way to the five-foot stone wall that marked the park's perimeter, and to skirt it until he reached Filbert Street. Below him, then, he could make out faint glimmers of house lights through gaps in the wind-driven whorls of mist. The cobblestones were littered with bits and pieces of refuse, and as he hurried along, the old rhyme about Telegraph Hill flicked unbidden across his mind.

The Irish, they live at the top of it,
The Italians, they live at the base of it;
And old tin cans, and kettles and pans,
Are scattered all over the face of it.

Drifter's Alley was half a block downhill. If he hadn't known its location, he might have missed it: there were no streetlights here, the signpost at the intersection was obscured, and the alley's narrow mouth yawned as black as the devil's fundament. The lane was unpaved; even though he moved slowly, he stumbled once on the uneven ground, muttered a curse under his breath when he nearly lost his balance. He might have been moving through a sinuous gray vacuum, for the only sounds were the distant fog warnings from the big bass diaphone on Alcatraz. Nor were there any lights to guide him.

Ahead the first of the two cottages took shape. Dark, dilapidated, its chimney canted at a drunken angle from a sagging roof. Untenanted, possibly abandoned. He passed it by, moving abreast of the vacant lot. The lot's expanse was choked with weeds and debris, bordered on its far end by a high, broken black wall that materialized into a clump of pepper trees. The second cottage was invisible behind them.

Quincannon left the narrow roadway, angling into the lot toward the copse. The mist muffled the sounds of his progress; he could scarcely hear his own footsteps. The pungent pepper scent sharpened as he moved in among the trees. Through an opening between two of them, then, he could make out the second cottage.

He stood there for a time to tab up the place and get the lay. It was another ram-shackle specimen as forlorn-looking as the first, with no lamplight showing and no sign of activity inside or out. Either Jack Travers was already in bed asleep, an unlikely prospect at this early hour — it couldn't be much past nine o'clock — or else he was a night creature, like the vampires of legend, and out somewhere spending a portion of his ill-gotten gains. If the former, Quincannon would surprise him in his bed, put the grab on him, and if necessary, do a bit of skull-dragging to lay hands on the stolen Wells, Fargo money. If the latter, he would search the premises for the green-and-greasy, and whether he found it or not, await Travers's return.

He drew the Navy, then eased out of the tree-heavy darkness. Cans, bottles, other detritus were strewn among the weeds growing in the side yard, and there were holes and mounds of dirt here and there as if someone had been digging with a spade. He managed to avoid all the obstacles until he was but a few yards from the cottage's side wall, when the toe of his boot stubbed against something that made a rattling, clanging noise in the stillness. He froze in place, tensed, listening. The sound had been loud enough to carry a short distance, but it produced no response from inside. The silence that followed remained unbroken.

Quincannon waited several more seconds before he continued forward, bypassing more holes and piles of dirt. A window in the side wall was shuttered; the narrow front porch had the kind of tumbledown look that meant rotted boards that would squeak loudly when trod upon. Stealthily he changed direction and made his way around to the rear, past a tangle of berry bushes and a privy that looked as if it were about to topple over sideways. No porch there, just an irregular path leading from a rear door to the privy.

He crept along the path to the door, half expecting to find it barred from within. But when he tried the latch, it moved freely and the door opened an inch or two, the hinges making no sound. He paused again to listen, heard nothing from inside, and eased the door inward far enough to edge his big body through.

The room he was in was small and cramped; the outlines of a table, a standing cupboard, a cast-iron stove identified it as a kitchen. Again he stood with ears straining, and again heard only silence. Always sensitive to the presence of others in places of darkness, familiar and unfamiliar, he felt none of the warning signs here. The place was empty.

Nevertheless, he continued to hold the Navy at the ready while with his left hand he removed a lucifer from his vest pocket, snapped it alight with his thumbnail. The flickering glow showed him a room in disarray: the cupboard drawers pulled out and emptied, chairs overturned, the floor and tabletop littered with broken dishes, scattered sticks of firewood, food remnants a-crawl with insects. He followed the light through a doorway into another, larger front room. This one was in an even greater state of upheaval, the floor strewn with overturned and smashed furniture, a coal stove spilling ashes through its open door, a crumpled carpet shoved into a corner. Floorboards had been pried up in several different places, leaving large gaps.

Another doorway stood to his left, covered with the remnants of a bead curtain: the bedroom, the only other room in a cottage of this size. The lucifer burned down and went out before Quincannon reached the curtain; he produced and struck another. The combined odors of sulfur and the night's chill, damp mist were sharp in the air, but as he approached the curtain, a new and far less tolerable smell came to him — one that he knew all too well. He shouldered through the curtain, causing the beads to click violently.

The match flame, held high, revealed more evidence of a frenzied search. A half-overturned cot had nothing on it but a soiled blanket. But on a second cot against the wall opposite —

The dead man was sprawled on his back, fully dressed, mouth and eyes agape. Quincannon stepped closer. The black-dried blood on the corpse's shirtfront had become a meal for flies and ants. Shot once at close range with a large caliber weapon, judging by the size of the wound. At least three and possibly four days ago, he judged.

A third match revealed the dead man to

have been in his early thirties, wiry, dark, balding, without facial hair that might have concealed a mole the size of a dime at a corner of his mouth. He was no one Quincannon had seen before. Jack Travers? Or whoever had torn the cottage apart, caught in the act and dispatched for his troubles?

The reason for the search seemed obvious: the Wells, Fargo loot. Had Travers had an accomplice, or had someone gotten wind of his and the money's whereabouts and come to hijack it? Not Bob Cantwell, else he wouldn't have confided the address to a stranger for a mere one hundred dollars. But possibly another party he'd told about this house for a cash settlement. One shot fired in any case, unheard because of the cottage's relative isolation, and the shooter long gone with or without the spoils.

Hell and damn!

Quincannon holstered his weapon, breathing through his mouth. An oil lamp lay on the floor, its globe unbroken; he picked it up and lighted the wick, then went to the cot. The dead man's clothing was disarranged, trouser and shirt pockets turned out and empty. A scatter of items that come from those pockets were on the cot and the floor beneath it. So was a wicked-looking spring blade knife, its sharp surfaces free of stains — poor defense against a pistol.

A cheap pocket watch told him nothing; the inside lid bore no inscription. Neither did the other items he found: a coin purse containing two dimes, a nickel, and four pennies; the stub of a pencil; several pieces of hard candy; a sack of Bull Durham; and two well-pawed French postcards that Quincannon studied judiciously in the lamplight before discarding.

A new-looking frock coat had been tossed into a corner. Its pockets and lining had been ripped apart, but he picked it up and examined it nonetheless. And a good thing he took nothing for granted, for the searcher had missed something that Quincannon's deft fingers detected — a folded piece of paper that must have slipped through a pocket hole and lodged in the lining of one of the tails. Scrawled on the paper in penmanship so poor as to be barely identifiable was: *The Kid, 9:15, Tuesday, usual place.*

The paper hadn't been there long; didn't look old and wasn't worn. Was the Kid, whoever he was, the murderer? Or did the name apply to Bob Cantwell? And had Cantwell lied or withheld information about the scope of his involvement in the robbery?

Grimly, Quincannon refolded and pocketed the paper. No matter who had committed this crime and where he might have gone, he would not get away with it or with Wells, Fargo's $35,000 if the swag was now in his possession. Quincannon had chased down miscreants the length and breadth of California, across a dozen states and territories. He would, as he had once declaimed to Sabina, pursue a quarry to the ends of the earth, even into the bowels of the Pit if necessary. Few had escaped him, none that he would admit to publicly — and none at all when it meant the collection of a reward as substantial as $3,500.

Glowering, he blew out the lamp and made a hurried exit through the unlatched front door. On his way to track down the cowardly little weasel who had sent him to Drifter's Alley.

5
QUINCANNON

There was no sign of Bob Cantwell at the Bucket of Beer Saloon. And neither the bartender nor the handful of remaining customers could or would say where the young rascal might have gone to gamble away his one hundred-dollar windfall. Quincannon tarried long enough to drink two cups of hot clam broth, his favorite tipple; his blood had thinned considerably since his discovery in Drifter's Alley and the night's chill had cut into him bone-deep. His earlier exhilaration was gone, his mood now considerably darker.

It turned darker still when he discovered that Cantwell had not as yet returned to his room at Drake's Rest. The front door of the lodging house was unlocked, the crone having carelessly forgotten to lock it, or else it was intentionally left off the latch so she wouldn't have to admit late-arriving tenants who had misplaced their keys. No lamp burned in the common room or anywhere else inside; Quincannon had to burn another lucifer to light his way upstairs and locate the door with a painted numeral 3 on it. Locked, that one, and no sounds from within or response to his knuckle rap on the panel.

Downstairs again, he paused in the hallway. There was nothing to be gained in doing any more tramping around the area; for all he knew Cantwell had gone uptown to do his rolling of the bones at Riley's House of Chance. But he was loath to put off his second conversation with the clerk until tomorrow; in all cases he preferred to strike while the iron was hot, the more so in situations such as this one. He thumbed another match alight to consult his stemwinder. Nearly eleven o'clock. Tomorrow being a workday, it was likely that Cantwell, win or lose, would return before it got to be too late. A wait of an hour or even two, Quincannon decided, wouldn't try his patience too severely. And he had no compunction about doing so on the premises, uninvited.

He followed the match flame into the common room, where he took the liberty of lighting a small oil lamp. His presence disturbed the scrawny parrot, whose cage was now covered with a black cloth; the bird made rustling and muttering noises before subsiding again. Quincannon sat in a lumpy, dusty armchair and settled down to his vigil.

A creeping weariness from his night's exertions, the lateness of the hour, and the house's stillness combined after a while to put him into a long doze. But the sounds of the front door opening and footsteps in the hallway brought him instantly alert. He was on his feet and moving when Bob Cantwell came into his line of sight.

The self-pitying look on the youth's face said that he'd had no more luck than usual with the dice tonight. When he saw Quincannon approaching, sudden fright replaced the self-pity and he backed up a step, his body stiffening, his hands lifting as if to ward off an attack.

"You," he said. "What . . . what're you doing here?"

"We need to have another talk, Bob."

"Why? I've already told you all I know —"

"Have you? I doubt it." Quincannon caught his arm, tugged him into the common room. Cantwell tried in vain to pull away.

"Don't hurt me! If you try I'll shout the house down —"

"Tell me what Jack Travers looks like."

". . . What?"

"Your cousin, Jack Travers. Describe him."

"I don't . . . what's the idea? Why do you want to know that?"

Quincannon fixed him with a steely eye and pinched his arm more tightly. "Describe him, Bob."

"Lean, hard . . . black hair . . . clean-shaven . . ."

"Large mole at one side of his mouth?"

"Yes. A mole, yes."

"Now tell me about 'the Kid.' "

Cantwell blinked, blinked again. "Kid? What kid?"

"The one your cousin was meeting regularly at the same place."

"I don't know what you're talking about." But he did know. The furtive shift of his eyes, the sudden tenseness of his body, testified to that.

"You, Bob? Are you the Kid?"

"No! I told you, I haven't seen Jack Travers since I gave him the key to the cottage —"

"What was your role in the robbery?"

"My . . . None! I had nothing to do with it! I'm a respectable —"

"But the Kid did, eh? Who is he?"

"I . . . I don't have any idea."

"I think you do."

"Jack never said anything to me about a

kid. Why're you asking me all these questions? Why don't you go up to Drifter's Alley and ask him?"

"I've already been to Drifter's Alley," Quincannon said. "Your cousin was there, but he couldn't tell me anything."

"Why couldn't he?"

"He's dead. Shot. And the cottage torn apart by whoever killed him."

Cantwell's eyes bugged wide. His mouth opened and closed, opened and closed, not unlike a gaffed sea bass.

"Jack Travers killed? Oh, my God! But it couldn't have been —"

"Couldn't have been whom?"

Cantwell wagged his head. Then his body spasmed, stiffened, as if he'd been struck by a sudden thought, and a name burst out of him unbidden. "Zeke!"

"Zeke, eh? Who would he be?"

"No. Oh, God, no! Suppose that big bastard comes after *me* next?"

"Why would he, if you had nothing to do with the robbery?"

Another head wag. In the lamplight Cantwell's face was the color of clabbered milk.

Quincannon said, "If that were his intention you'd already be dead. Travers was shot three or four days ago —"

But Cantwell wasn't listening. A surge of panic had him in its grip, and it served to double his strength. He struggled mightily, managed to break loose from the tight-fingered grip on his arm. Quincannon clutched at him, caught the tail of his coat as he turned away, but couldn't hold it; Cantwell twisted away and ran for the front door.

In the darkness and his haste to give chase, Quincannon stumbled over a fold in the threadbare carpet and banged into and upset a table. By the time he regained his balance Cantwell was out the door and gone. The noise caused by the falling table woke the parrot, which began screeching maniacally in its cage. This in turn woke some of the house's other residents; angry cries followed Quincannon as he lurched outside.

It took him a few seconds to locate Cantwell in the foggy darkness. The youth was twenty rods distant, fleeing in a spindle-legged run along the sidewalk. "Stop!" Quincannon yelled. "Come back here, you damned young scruff!"

The shout had no effect. Cantwell didn't even break stride, running head down as if a demon from hell were breathing fire on his backside. Quincannon gave chase, but couldn't catch him. It was all he could do to maintain enough speed to keep him in sight.

Cantwell dashed diagonally across the empty street in mid-block, casting a brief look back over his shoulder. The nearness of Quincannon's pursuit spurred him past the darkened front of a warehouse and into an alley beyond its board-fenced side yard. The fog not only hid him then, but deadened the pound of his footsteps. Furious now, Quincannon charged around the corner of the fence without slowing. It was like hurling himself into a vat of India ink; wet black closed around him and he could see nothing but vague shapes through the ragged coils and streamers of mist. He slowed, heard only silence, plunged ahead —

Something swung out of the murk, struck him squarely across the left temple, and knocked him over like a ninepin.

It was not the first time he had been hit on or about the head, and his skull had withstood harder blows without serious damage or loss of consciousness. He didn't lose consciousness now, though for a few seconds his thoughts rattled around like pebbles in a tin can. Through a faint ringing in his ears he heard Cantwell's frightened voice cry something unintelligible, then a clatter on the cobbles nearby — a board or whatever it was that had been used to bludgeon him. He rolled over onto his knees and forearms, hoisted himself unsteadily to his feet. Fresh pain throbbed in his temple. Somewhere in the darkness ahead there was again the faint beat of receding footfalls.

A multijointed oath swelled his throat. He bit it back and plunged onward, shaking his head to clear it, using the fence to guide him and heedless of obstacles. Blood trickled warm and sticky down his right cheek, adding fuel to his outrage.

The fog-softened steps veered off to the right, were replaced by scraping sounds, resumed dimly at a greater distance. Quincannon's mental processes steadied. There must be a second alley that crossed this one through the middle of the block. He slowed, saw the intersection materialize through the gray vapors, and swung himself around into the new passage.

Where, after half a dozen paces, he ran into another wooden fence.

He caromed off, staggering. The multijointed oath once more swelled his throat and this time two of the smokier words slipped out. He threw himself back to the fence, caught the top and scaled its six-foot height. When he dropped down on the far side he could hear Cantwell's steps a little more clearly. The fog was patchier here; he was able to see all the way to the dull shine of an electric streetlamp on Howard Street beyond. A running shadow was just blending into other shadows there, heading toward the Embarcadero.

When he reached the corner he skidded to a halt, breathing in thick wheezes. Visibility was still good; he could make out Cantwell's thin shape less than half a block away. He broke into another run, summoning reserves that lengthened his strides; he was less than thirty rods behind when the youth crossed Beale Street. Gaining on him, by Godfrey! Quincannon raced across Beale. But as he came up onto the sidewalk on the opposite side, his quarry once more disappeared.

Another blasted alley, this one dirt-floored, he saw as he reached its mouth. He turned into it with considerably more caution than he'd entered the previous pair. No ambush this time: Cantwell was still fleeing. Quincannon plowed ahead, managed to reach the alley's far end without blundering into anything. There, he slowed long enough to determine that the footfalls were now fading away to his right, in the direction of Folsom Street. He angled that way, spied Cantwell some distance ahead — and then, again, lost sight of him. And when that happened, his footsteps were no longer audible.

The restless mist was thick-pocketed that way; the side lamps on a hansom cab at the far intersection were barely visible. At a fast walk now, Quincannon continued another ten paces. Close by, then, he heard the nervous neighing of a horse, followed by a similar sound from a second horse. A few more paces, and the faint glow of a lantern materialized. Another, slender wedge of yellow appeared on the right. One of the horses nickered again, and harness leather creaked. He heard nothing else.

He kept moving until he could identify the sources of the light. One came from a lantern mounted on a large brewery wagon drawn by two dray animals that filled the alley, the other from a partially open door to the building on the right — a two-story brick structure with an overhanging balcony at the second level. Above the door was a sign whose lettering was just discernible: MCKENNA'S ALE HOUSE.

The wagon was laden with medium-sized kegs, which indicated a late delivery to the saloon. There was no sign of anyone human, though he could hear the mutter of voices from inside. He drew closer, peering to the right because that direction offered the largest amount of space for passage around the wagon.

The thrown object came from his left. Quincannon saw it — one of the kegs — in time to pitch his body sideways against the ale house wall. The keg sailed past his head, missing him by precious little, slammed into the bricks above and broke apart. He threw his arm up to protect his head as staves and metal strapping and the contents of the keg rained down on him.

The foamy brew, a green and pungent lager, drenched him from head to foot, got into his eyes and mouth and nose. Spluttering, he pawed at his face and shook his head like a bewildered bull. Once again he heard the pound of retreating footfalls, which impelled him to continue the chase. But in his haste to get past the wagon, his foot slipped on the beer-muddied ground. Down he went on his backside, sliding forward so that he was nearly brained by one of the frightened dray horses' plunging hooves.

The rear door to McKenna's Ale House opened as he struggled upright and a pair of curious heads poked out. Quincannon, giving vent now to most of his vocabulary of cuss words, drew and brandished the Navy and the heads disappeared so swiftly that they might never have been there at all. He slid along the bricks, rubbing at his beer-stung eyes. The dray horses were still shuffling around in harness, though neither was plunging any longer. He finally managed to shove past them, stumbled out onto Folsom Street.

The fog rolling up from the waterfront was as thick here as Creole gumbo. All he could hear was the ever-present clanging of fog bells. All he could see was empty damp-swirled darkness.

Cantwell, damn his cowardly eyes, had vanished again. And this time there was no picking up his trail.

6
SABINA

She spooned some of the glutinous, evil-smelling food that her cat, Adam, loved into his saucer and set it down on the kitchen floor. Happy rumbles came from the sharp-eared, long-tailed Abyssinian and Siamese mixture; his short golden fur rippled with pleasure as he tucked into his feast.

Better you than I, Sabina thought.

From her small icebox she took a piece of fresh tuna, placed it in another saucer, and set that on the outside porch for old Annie, the homeless woman. Annie would not come for her breakfast until Sabina had left the flat, but she would already be waiting and watching close by.

A cup of morning coffee sat cooling on the counter. Sabina took it to the parlor and sat in the Morris chair there to reflect once more on the bewildering events of the previous night.

After she, Mayor Sutro, David St. Ives,

and Dr. Bowers had returned to the Heights from their futile search along the Great Highway, they had enlisted the aid of servants and some of the male party guests in a thorough canvass of the grounds by lantern light. That had also proved futile, as she knew it would. Virginia St. Ives was not to be found on Sutro Heights, just as her body had not been found on the Great Highway. No matter what anyone might think — and there was skepticism among others besides the girl's brother — Sabina had not been mistaken in what she'd witnessed on the overlook. The ghostlike figure on the parapet, its leap, the scream, the sound of the body tumbling down the cliff — all of that had happened just as she remembered it.

The question of what had become of Virginia's body was puzzling. But so was the reason for her death leap. The suicide note was ambiguous and offered no hint as to what would compel a lovely, rich post-debutante with the most promising of futures to commit such a drastic act.

Unrequited love was one possibility, a serious illness another. A third was pregnancy out of wedlock.

Adam sauntered in and jumped onto Sabina's lap. She stroked him absently as he settled down to wash his face and paws.

Would the fact that the girl had been forbidden to see Lucas Whiffing be sufficient cause? It didn't seem likely. Once her parents returned from Sacramento, they couldn't have expected Sabina or anyone else to spend days on end watching over their daughter; there were any number of ways she could have continued to keep company with the boy.

Illness seemed just as improbable. Virginia had been too pink-cheeked and clear-eyed, too energetic, to be suffering from a severe malady. There were moments, in fact, when she had seemed to glow. . . .

Didn't cousin Callie and her friends describe women who were with child as glowing? Yes, but those discussed pregnancies had occurred within wedlock and in all cases the children were wanted. If Virginia's glow had been the result of pregnancy, it was probable she and Lucas would have wanted the baby, and as was usual in such circumstances, the St. Ives's would eventually have accepted their grandchild, if not Lucas as their son-in-law. Virginia would have had no cause to take her unborn baby's life as well as her own.

But the situation might have been far more dire than it appeared on the surface.

If Virginia had indeed tossed her bonnet over the windmill and found herself in a family way, and Lucas Whiffing had refused to marry her, death might have seemed preferable to facing shame and social banishment. She wouldn't be the first or the last eighteen-year-old girl in trouble to make that senseless decision.

The door chimes sounded.

Now who could that be at this early hour? She set down her coffee cup, brushed Adam off her lap, and went to peer through a parting in the draperies that covered the windows overlooking the street. Two men, one bare-headed, the other wearing a felt slouch hat, stood in the vestibule. She recognized the little chubby one in the derby: Homer Keeps, a muckraking journalist with the *Evening Bulletin.* The other man would undoubtedly be a reporter as well. She might have known that the press would catch wind of the tragedy at Sutro Heights, despite the mayor's desire that the story not be made public, and come haring to her with a barrage of questions and insinuations.

Sabina was in no frame of mind for such harassment this early in the day. Quickly she caught up the reticule in which she'd put cousin Callie's ruined gown and slip-

pers, snatched her jacket from the hall tree
— last night's fog had mostly burned off
and the weather would be sunny and mild
enough for a light wrap — and hurried
through the kitchen to the back door. Down
a short flight of steps and she was in the
rear yard, which was screened from the
street in front by trees and shrubbery. A gate
in the black-iron fence beyond the carriage
house led to an alleyway that bisected the
block. She made her way along there to the
next cross street and then downhill. It was
still too early to venture downtown; she
boarded a westbound cable car instead.

The handsome Victorian Callie French
shared with her husband was in the fashion-
able neighborhood just beyond Van Ness
Avenue. Sabina surprised her plump blond-
haired cousin by her early arrival, and
surprised her even more when she presented
her with what was left of the borrowed garments. "My Lord," Callie exclaimed, "these
look as if you were playing outdoor tag
instead of attending a ball last night."

"I was, more or less," Sabina said ruefully.

She apologized profusely for the damaged
garments, but Callie waved it away. "Stuff
and nonsense. The gown was too small for
me anyway. What happened?"

79

"It's a long story. You'll no doubt read about it in the newspapers tonight."

"The newspapers? Oh, my! You haven't gotten yourself in some sort of trouble, have you? And at one of the mayor's parties, of all places?"

"In a manner of speaking, yes, but through no fault of my own."

"Did something happen with the young woman you were watching?"

"To her, yes."

"Well? *What,* for heaven's sake?"

"That is what I intend to find out."

"Pshaw! You're being very mysterious."

"I don't mean to be. It's just that I haven't time to discuss the matter right now — I have an appointment downtown." Which wasn't quite true, but close enough to her intention. "I only stopped by to return the gown and slippers and to apologize. We'll have a luncheon soon and I'll tell you everything in detail."

F. W. Ellerby's bicycle and sporting goods emporium was on Powell Street a few doors off Market. The space it occupied was small — an uptown business district showroom rather than a full-sized store. Its plate-glass front window displayed three bicycles — a man's, a woman's, and a tandem — and a

80

small selection of other items artfully arranged to attract the attention of passersby. It had just opened for business when Sabina arrived.

The showroom's interior was crowded with several more bicycles and a wide range of sporting goods, from firearms to archery and croquet sets to a colorful array of kites. The first employee Sabina encountered was a heavy-set, middle-aged man dressed in a rather garish flower-patterned waistcoat. When she asked for Lucas Whiffing he said somewhat stiffly, "I am not sure if Mr. Whiffing is here today — I've only just arrived. Illness or whatever may have kept him home yet another day this week. But I'll see."

Mr. Whiffing was there, having apparently just come in himself. The young man who emerged through a doorway at the rear and approached her was more conservatively dressed than his fellow employee, small of stature, and darkly handsome except for a haggard look around the eyes that might have been the result of recent illness or a simple lack of sleep. The smile he wore under a narrow waxed mustache was the boyishly charming sort Sabina instinctively distrusted. It was the first time she had set eyes on him, though he had been described to her by Virginia St. Ives's mother. Mrs. St. Ives considered him "a slick and devious fortune hunter," though she seemed never to have met him, either. Whether or not the appraisal was apt remained to be seen.

"Yes, Madam, what may I do for you?"

"My name is Sabina Carpenter." She presented him with one of her cards. "I'd like to speak to you privately, Mr. Whiffing."

"I don't understand," he said when he finished peering at the card. "A woman investigator?"

"You find something wrong with that?"

"Wrong? No, not at all. What is it you wish to speak to me about?"

"Virginia St. Ives."

His only reaction was a wry twist to his smile. He seemed not to know yet of the girl's suicide or the strange disappearance of her body. Nor to have recognized Sabina's name.

"What about Ms. St. Ives?"

"In private, please. It's important."

"Well . . . Mr. Ellerby doesn't like employees using his office when he isn't here, but we can talk in the storeroom." He ushered her through the rear doorway and into a narrow room lined with well-filled shelves and redolent of leather, rubber, and linseed oil. "If you'd like to sit down, Miss Carpenter, I can fetch a chair —"

"Mrs. Carpenter. No, that isn't necessary. I'm afraid I have some bad news for you about Virginia St. Ives, if you haven't already been informed."

"Virginia? No. Has something happened to her?"

"I'm afraid so." Briefly and with a minimum of detail she told him what had happened the night before.

He reacted with shock, bewilderment, distress — all of it seemingly genuine. He leaned heavily against one of the shelves, shaking his head, his eyes moist and glistening. "My God, are you certain she couldn't have survived the fall? If her body wasn't found, then she might still be alive. . . ."

"I can't explain the missing body, but no, it's virtually impossible for her to have survived such a plunge."

"But why would she do such a thing? She was so young, so full of life. . . ."

"You have no idea?"

"No. Absolutely none."

"I've been told you and she were quite close."

"We were keeping company, yes, until her parents refused to allow her to see me any longer." A touch of bitterness underlay the grief in his voice. "They consider me beneath her station. 'A lowly clerk who lives in the squalor of Carville,' in her father's words. I may be only a clerk and stockboy at present, but Mr. Ellerby is planning to open a second store and has promised to make me manager. And whatever Carville may be, it's certainly not squalid. . . ." He broke off, scrubbed his face with his palms.

Sabina asked, "How serious was your relationship with Miss St. Ives?"

"Not as serious as it might have become had we been permitted more time together. I may one day have asked her to be my wife."

"But it hadn't reached that stage of intimacy yet?"

"No. If only she hadn't listened to her father . . ." The hands came down and he frowned at Sabina as if just struck by a thought. "I suppose he's the one who hired you. To make sure Virginia didn't disobey his orders."

"While he and his wife were away in Sacramento, yes."

"Why were you chaperoning her last night? Did you think Virginia might try to sneak off to meet me somewhere?"

"I didn't think anything, Mr. Whiffing. I was merely attending to my duties."

"Not attending to them well, if you weren't able to prevent her from hurling herself off that cliff."

"I had no idea what she was planning to do. I truly wish I had."

"So do I." He sighed heavily. "Oh, God, poor Virginia," he said then. "She was . . . downhearted the last time I saw her, but I thought it was because she'd been forced to end our relationship."

"That was at your meeting at Coppa's Restaurant last week?"

"Yes. She said she couldn't go against her father's wishes, that he would disown her if she did. I was more upset than she was, at least outwardly."

At the breakup itself, Sabina wondered, or at the end of his chances of marrying into a considerable fortune?

Lucas said, "But she must have been depressed, deeply depressed about something else to do what she did. I can't imagine that it had anything to do with me."

"She gave no indication of what it might have been?"

"None. I would have questioned her if she had."

"Did you have any contact with her after that day?"

"No. I kept hoping she would change her

mind, try to get in touch with me, but she didn't."

"Do you know if she was seeing anyone else?"

He shook his head. "If she was, it was at the forceful urging of her parents. But I don't believe she was. At least not during the time we were together."

"And how long was that?"

"Three months."

"How did you and she meet?"

"She came in one morning to view our new line of bicycles. Our conversation was friendly enough so that I was encouraged to invite her to a noon-hour stroll through Union Square, and she agreed. I bought her a corsage at old Giovanni's stand — pansies, her favorites."

"How often did you meet after that?"

"Whenever my job and her busy schedule permitted. Public places. The little tea room in Maiden Lane, restaurants where it's permitted for young women of her station to dine alone with gentlemen. The Chutes Amusement Park on one occasion, Golden Gate Park on another."

"Always just the two of you? Or did you share some of these outings with others of your acquaintance or hers?"

"Just the two of us. I was never introduced

to anyone in her circle, but that was not because she was in any way ashamed of me." Lucas said this defensively. "The opportunity simply never arose."

"Did you spend an entire day, well into the evening, in her company?"

"No. Our outings lasted no more than two or three hours."

"Were you ever alone together in private circumstances?"

"Private circumstances? No, never. Why would you ask that?"

"I'm sure you realize one possible reason for Virginia's despondent state is that she found herself caught in a shameful situation—"

Color came into Lucas's cheeks; he drew himself up angrily. "Are you suggesting that she might have been with child and I the father? That is an insulting and completely false notion, Mrs. Carpenter. Virginia and I were never intimate, never exchanged more than a chaste kiss."

The truth? Or was he protesting too much? "Pregnancy by another man might still be the cause."

"I refuse to believe that. Virginia could be gay and impulsive at times, but underneath she was an extremely virtuous young lady. I don't care how many beaux she had, she would have remained pure until her wedding night."

Sabina wasn't so sure, but she saw no reason to argue the point. It would not have done her any good to try; Lucas ended the interview abruptly, saying that he didn't feel well and needed a breath of air, and leaving her to find her own way out through the front of the store.

A curious young man, Lucas Whiffing. His answers to her questions had seemed honest enough, and yet Sabina was left with the feeling that he hadn't been completely straightforward with her. Either he was an habitual liar, or he knew and was hiding something for reasons of his own. Or both.

Virginia St. Ives had many friends her age, but evidently only one close enough to have been a confidante — Grace DeBrett, the girl whom Sabina had met at the St. Ives home and who had been at the mayor's party last night. Miss DeBrett lived with her family in a Nob Hill mansion, Sabina's destination by hansom cab after leaving F. W. Ellerby's.

Grace was home, and the maid who answered the door took Sabina's card in to her. And brought it back in less than two minutes. "Miss DeBrett does not wish to see you and requests that you do not call here again," she said, and closed the door firmly in Sabina's face.

7
QUINCANNON

Quincannon's humor was black and smoldering when he left his rooms Saturday morning. In addition to the indignities he had suffered the night before — a mushy and painful wound on his temple where Bob Cantwell had clubbed him, a knot on his forehead from his collision with the fence, torn and beer-drenched clothing, and despite a bath, the faint lingering scent of a derelict — he had spent a mostly sleepless night. Cantwell would pay and pay dear when he got his hands on the little weasel. A $3,500 reward for professional services rendered was all well and good, but there were also satisfactions to be had in repaying thumps and lumps in kind.

Hammond Realtors, Battery Street, was not open for business — a slipshod operation, in Quincannon's opinion, if its doors remained closed on Saturdays. From there he went to Drake's Rest, but Cantwell had not returned to the lodging house even long enough to gather up his belongings. Yet another silver dollar bribe to the harridan owner bought Quincannon entry to Cantwell's room, which he searched quickly and fruitlessly. There was nothing there to suggest where the young fool might have fled to, or to further link him to the Wells, Fargo Express robbery and the whereabouts of the man named Zeke and the missing money.

His next stop was the Western Union office, where he sent a wire to Clem Holloway at the Holloway Detective Agency in Los Angeles requesting information on Jack Travers — current address, criminal record, any known alliances in San Francisco. He and Holloway had exchanged business favors in the past; Clem knew almost as much about the Southern California underworld as Quincannon did about Northern California's, and would respond with all possible dispatch.

Quincannon's mood continued to darken as the morning progressed. A visit to Ezra Bluefield at the Scarlet Lady proved futile; the deadfall owner could tell him nothing about Cantwell or Jack Travers, or who the Kid or Zeke might be, the monikers being not uncommon among Barbary Coast and

91

other underworld denizens. Bluefield promised to put the word out on Cantwell, but without his usual enthusiasm. Favors as repayment for the debts he owed only went so far for a man of his hard-bitten temperament — even more hardbitten since his unsuccessful bid to purchase a more respectable saloon in the Uptown Tenderloin — and it was plain that he was beginning to feel put upon. Quincannon warned himself to be careful not to ask too much too often in the future.

During his years with the U.S. Secret Service and then as a private investigator, he had made the acquaintance of a long list of minor criminals, both in and out of the Barbary Coast, who were willing to peddle information for cash. But he had no more luck with any of these he managed to locate. Not even the most reliable, the bunco steerer known as Breezy Ned and the "blind" newspaper vendor called Slewfoot, had any information for him. Nor did Charles Riley at the House of Chance. Riley had not seen Cantwell since the clerk's abortive attempt to sell him information about the Wells, Fargo robbery in exchange for gambling credit; wherever Cantwell had gone to roll the bones the night before, it had not been to the Tenderloin.

Quincannon had his lunch, as he often did, at Hoolihan's Saloon on Second Street. Hoolihan's had been his favorite watering hole during his drinking days and he continued to patronize it because it was an honest place, both staff and regular customers friendly, a challenging game of pool or billiards could always be had, and the free lunch was of a higher standard than many. Usually his appetite was prodigious; in his present gloomy state, he managed to down only two corned beef-and-cheese sandwiches and three briny pickles with his customary cup of clam juice.

As he was finishing the second sandwich, Ben Joyce, the head barman, approached him. "Well, you bloody Scotsman, I see you and your partner are back in the public eye. But with a black one of your own this time, eh?"

"What are you nattering about?"

"The queer business with your partner at the mayor's home last night."

Quincannon felt a twist of alarm. "*What queer business?*"

"Don't tell me you don't know. It's front page news in the latest edition of the *Evening Bulletin.*"

"I haven't seen that blasted scandal sheet. Bring me a copy, if you have one."

Ben Joyce had one and brought it. The headlines were prominent:

FANTASTIC OCCURANCE AT MAYOR'S HOME

WOMAN DETECTIVE CLAIMS SOCIALITE LEAPT TO DEATH SUICIDE NOTE BUT NO BODY FOUND

The story that followed, penned by an inflammatory yellow journalist named Homer Keeps with whom Quincannon shared a strong mutual dislike, was even more puzzling and infuriating. The socialite whose alleged suicidal plunge from the Sutro Heights overlook was Virginia St. Ives, the young debutante Sabina had been hired to watch over. No one seemed able to explain why a careful search of the Great Highway below the cliff had failed to locate the girl's body. Sabina remained steadfast in her claim that she had witnessed the plunge, one which no one could have survived. David St. Ives, the girl's outraged brother, claimed that no matter what had happened, Sabina had been "severely negligent" in her watchdog duties. Homer Keeps inferred agreement, and had the audacity to add another, gratuitous insult: "Mrs. Carpenter and her flamboyant partner, John H. Quincannon," he wrote, "are well known among the lower classes of our city, in the past having reportedly indulged in business practices of a questionable nature."

Quincannon slammed the newspaper down so hard on the bar that glasses jumped and heads swiveled all along its length. After which he kicked a spittoon for good measure. Flamboyant! Well-known among the lower classes! Business practices of a questionable nature! As if these borderline libelous slurs were not injurious enough to his and Sabina's professional reputation, the bloody swine had deliberately — and it was surely deliberate — misprinted his middle initial. H. indeed. John *Frederick* Quincannon was not about to stand for such sly calumny.

From Hoolihan's he went straight to the Market Street offices of Carpenter and Quincannon, Professional Detective Services. His rage had calmed to a slow simmer by the time he got there, but it kindled quickly when he found a newshound from the *Chronicle* waiting for him with a string of annoying questions. He growled his refusal to be interviewed, and when the reporter persisted, Quincannon turned on the full force of his freebooter's glower and loomed threateningly until he beat a hasty retreat.

The fact that the office door was locked did nothing to improve his disposition. The lack of any message on his desk indicated that Sabina had yet to put in an appearance today. Confound it, why not? He believed none of the David St. Ives claptrap about her having been derelict in her duties last evening, but before he took steps to repair the damage done, he needed to have her version of what had happened.

He was at his desk, fidgeting and smoldering while he sifted through the day's mail, when the door opened. But it was not Sabina who entered. Nor was it a prospective client or any other visitor who would have been polite enough to knock first. No, it was the last person on earth he wished to see, this day or any day — a presence that set his blood to boiling again like the brew in a witch's cauldron.

The man who stood there smiling at him, gray cape flung over his narrow shoulders, walking stick in hand and deerstalker cap shading his hawkish countenance, was the pestiferous crackbrain who fancied himself to be Sherlock Holmes.

"Good afternoon, my good man. A pleasure to see you again, despite the present circumstances. It has been much too long since our last meeting."

"Not long enough." Quincannon glowered at him. "I thought you'd gone back to England or wherever you came from."

"I intended to return from the dead, as it were, yes, to resume my private inquiry practice in London and to put the good Dr. Watson's mind at ease. He believes me to have fallen victim to my arch enemy, Professor Moriarity, at Reichenbach Falls, if you recall, and I feel badly for having deceived the poor fellow. However, for personal reasons I have decided to remain 'deceased' and in your stimulating bailiwick awhile longer."

Stimulating bailiwick. Bah. "I suppose you're still sponging off Dr. Axminster."

"Sponging? Upon my soul, sir, you wound me grievously. I have never sponged, as you so quaintly put it, off anyone. I was a guest in Dr. Axminster's home for only a few weeks. In the interim since our last meeting, I have taken lodgings in several different places, under several different names, most recently in the Old Union Hotel."

Quincannon snorted. The Old Union was a less-than-genteel hostelry on the fringe of the Barbary Coast that catered to performers, traveling salesmen, and — evidently —

candidates for mental hospitals.

"I have not sought to renew our acquaintance until now," Holmes went on, "inasmuch as I have been engaged on a mission of the utmost secrecy and importance. The mission has been successfully accomplished for the most part, but of course I am still not at liberty to discuss it."

Bah and double bah. "Well? Why are you bothering me now?"

"Why, for purposes of commiseration, my dear chap. And to offer my services again, should you desire them."

"I don't desire them. Not today or ever again."

"Tut, tut," Holmes said, but his tone was one of tolerant comradeship. "It may well require my analytical powers as well as yours and the charming Mrs. Carpenter's to unravel last night's curious mystery at Mayor Sutro's estate. That is, *par foi,* if you and she have not yet deduced the correct answer."

"I haven't had time to deduce anything," Quincannon growled. "We haven't spoken yet today."

"Ah. So your knowledge of the young woman's strange disappearance comes from the same source as mine, the afternoon newspaper. All the more reason for us to join forces, wouldn't you say? Two preeminent detectives once again working in consort, now that a new game is afoot."

Quincannon studied the Englishman's neck, his fingers curled and his palms itching. Holmes or whatever his name had been a major irritant in a robbery, fraud, and murder investigation the previous year — what Quincannon referred to as the bughouse affair. Admittedly the addlepate had played a small role in the solution of the complicated case, purely through blind luck despite his claim of having used "observation, in particular observation of trifles, and deductive reasoning." The fact was, without Holmes's constant interference, the investigation would have been brought to a satisfactory conclusion much sooner. Sabina didn't agree, preferring to give the devil his due; she maintained that mad or not, the imposter had been surprisingly adept at employing the methods of his namesake. Poppycock! Not even the genuine Sherlock Holmes, if he were still alive and practicing, would have been able to outsleuth John Quincannon.

To still the strangler's urge in his hands, he proceeded to load tobacco into his stubby briar. Holmes took this as a tacit invitation to occupy the client's chair and charge his curved clay pipe. They regarded each other through clouds of mingled aromatic and putrid smoke, the Englishman still smiling, Quincannon still glowering.

At length Holmes said, "Well, John. May I call you John?"

"No."

"Shall we discuss our theories about last night's mystery?"

"Theories? What theories?"

"I have two. Surely you have hypothesized the same?"

"I told you, I haven't spoken to my partner today. How could I have any theories yet? All I know is what was written in the blasted newspaper."

"Which rather lurid account yielded two possible explanations for the evening's curious events, both perfectly sound, though of course neither may be the correct one. We must have more information before we can be certain of the truth."

Quincannon made an ominous rumbling sound in his throat. "I don't want to hear your damned theories. What did or didn't happen to Virginia St. Ives is none of your business and I'll thank you to keep your long nose out of it."

"Tut, tut," Holmes said mildly. "As you know from our past experience together,

I'm quite a tenacious fellow once I've caught the scent."

"You'll catch something else if you don't go away and leave me be. Can't you see I'm busy?"

Surprisingly, the bughouse Sherlock didn't put up any further argument. He said, "Ah, yes. As you wish, then," and got to his feet, taking his time about it; adjusted his cape, and made his way slowly to the door. But instead of walking through after he'd opened it, he turned, and said, "Before I take my leave, may I ask how your investigation is progressing?"

"What investigation?"

"The recent Wells, Fargo Express robbery."

This startled Quincannon enough to unhinge his jaw. "What makes you think I'm investigating that?"

"Three things I observed during our brief visit. No, four, counting the contusions on your forehead and temple."

"I don't know what the devil you're talking about."

Holmes smiled his enigmatic smile. "You needn't worry, John. I am merely an interested observer in that matter as in the one on Sutro Heights. I have no designs on the reward."

Quincannon said, somewhat lamely, "What reward?"

The answer was a widening of the smile and a broad wink. "If you should change your mind and decide to seek assistance or counsel, I shall remain at your service. The Union Hotel, room twelve." And with that, the Englishman was gone.

For several seconds Quincannon sat fuming and puzzling. A pox on the conceited twit! *What* three things had he observed, or was that balderdash? Yet he seemed to have guessed that the contusions were related to the Wells, Fargo investigation, and how was that possible? And how had he known about the reward? Quincannon refused to credit the Englishman with special deductive powers, but there was no gainsaying the fact that he had an uncanny knack for both guesswork and stumbling upon a surprising amount of covert information. It must have something to do with his derangement. Crackbrains could be very shrewd, especially one who claimed to be a famous deceased British detective.

The office was blue with smoke, most of it a foul leftover reek from the godawful tobacco Holmes preferred. Quincannon opened the window behind his desk, letting in a wind-driven swirl of fresh air and the clanging passage of cable cars on Market Street below. Then he finished opening the mail — not a single check, drat it — and was in the process of laboriously writing a report (he hated writing reports) on a recently concluded case when Sabina finally appeared.

"Oh, John," she said. "Good, I'm glad you're here."

"And I'm glad *you're* here. Where have you been?"

"Trying to make some sense of what happened last night. You know about that by now, I'm sure."

"From everyone but you, it seems."

"Yes, well, I'm sorry, but I thought you might not be in this morning and I wanted . . . oh, never mind." She looked and sounded frazzled as she shed her lamb's-wool coat, unpinned her hat, and hung both on the coatrack. "Have you been bothered by newspaper reporters?"

"Only one. And not for long."

"There'll be others, no doubt." Her nose wrinkled as she started toward her desk. "What's that dreadful smell? Not your usual pipe tobacco, is it?"

"No. A new blend." He had resolved not to tell her about the lunatic's unannounced and unwanted visit. It was of no importance

103

and she had enough on her mind as it was.

"Well, I hope you won't —" She broke off, peering at him more closely now. "John, your face. What happened to you?"

The concern in both her voice and her expression pleased him. "An accident of no consequence," he lied. He had also resolved not to burden her, just yet, with last night's misadventures on Telegraph Hill and along the waterfront. His wounded pride and dignity were still tender. When he did tell her, he would leave out some of the more embarrassing details.

Sabina was not fooled, however. She said, "You're a caution, John Quincannon. One of your nightly forays will be the death of you if you're not careful."

"You needn't worry about me, my dear. I'm well able to take care of myself."

"Are you? My husband said the same thing to me two nights before he was killed."

Sabina went to sit at her desk. A stray wisp of her high-coiled black hair come loose and was tickling her nose; she produced a hand mirror and proceeded to tuck and pin it back into place. Quincannon watched her avidly. As always, her dark blue eyes, high-cheekbone face, and comely figure quickened his pulses. He had never wanted for female companionship when he sought it, yet no woman had ever had quite the same effect on him as his partner. Part of it was unrequited passion, but his feelings for her ran deeper than simple desire. More deeply — and therefore more frustrating — with each passing day, it seemed.

When she finished fixing her hair, he said, "What exactly did happen at the mayor's soiree last night? The blasted newspaper account was somewhat sketchy on details. You had words with the St. Ives girl and followed her when she ran outside?"

"She had the words, not I. I thought she might have rushed out to meet her forbidden young swain, Lucas Whiffing."

"But instead she was bent on taking her life."

"Evidently. She met no one on the way, and I saw no one else on the overlook. At least no one near where she had climbed up onto the parapet. The fog was quite thick."

"How clearly did you see her on the wall?"

"Clearly enough. She had her back to me, facing the sea with her arms bent away from her body. A ghostlike figure in the mist." Sabina paused, little wrinkle lines appearing in the smooth skin of her forehead. "There was something . . . odd about the way she was standing there. It didn't strike me at the time, and yet when I think about it . . ."

"Odd in what way?"

"I can't quite put my finger on it. It was the next second or two that she jumped."

"You're certain she did jump, not slipped and fell?"

"It certainly looked as though she threw herself forward off the parapet. I heard her scream, then the sounds of her body sliding through the ice plant below the wall and over the edge."

"Yet there was no sign of her body on the Great Highway."

"None. Except for the scarf she was wearing, caught on a torn cypress limb."

"Then the only possible explanation is that someone came along, found her, and spirited her away alive or dead. Was there enough time for that to have happened?"

Sabina nodded. "Fifteen to twenty minutes had elapsed by the time I summoned the others and we started down to the highway. But it's an unlikely explanation. There was very little traffic because of the fog, the mayor's home is the only one in the immediate vicinity, and we met no one entering the grounds or driving on Point Lobos. If someone did happen along and picked up the body, where would it have been taken? Not to the nearest habitation south of the Heights, Dickey's Road House;

106

we inquired there. And what reason could anyone have had for transporting it any greater distance?"

"Isn't Carville where the Whiffing lad lives?"

"With his parents, yes. Even if by some bizarre happenstance he was on the Great Highway when she fell, he'd have no reason to take her all the way to his home. It's unlikely a doctor resides in Carville. There would hardly have been a need for one in any event."

"The girl couldn't possibly have survived the fall?"

"Of some two hundred and fifty feet? Hardly."

"So," Quincannon said, "a pretty riddle."

"Ugly riddle is more appropriate. And there's more to it than what happened to Virginia St. Ives's body."

"Indeed?"

"When she left the mansion, she took a circuitous route through the grounds rather than going straight to the overlook from the rear. I can't help wondering why."

"Did she know you were following her?"

"She must have. I made no attempt to keep her from seeing me."

"Didn't matter to her, then, because she believed you wouldn't be able to catch up and stop her."

"And I didn't," Sabina said with bitter regret.

"Not your fault. You couldn't have guessed what she had in mind. What do you suppose drove her to it?"

"I wish I knew. Whatever it was, it wasn't a spur-of-the-moment decision. The suicide note proves that."

"The usual reason young girls commit suicide, perhaps?"

"Pregnant, you mean? Yes, I thought of that. The child's father would most likely be Lucas Whiffing, in that case, and he would have had to refuse to marry her to put her in such dire straits. But he seemed genuinely shocked and upset when I spoke to him this morning. He claims their relationship was not as serious as the St. Ives believed. Denied they had been intimate, and appeared to resent the implication that she had been anything but virtuous."

"Men have been known to lie in such circumstances," Quincannon said mildly.

"Well, of course they have. Whether Lucas Whiffing is one of them is still open to question."

Nothing happened during the remainder of the afternoon to improve Quincannon's spirits. There were no visits or messages from any of his contacts. Twice he had to fend off tenacious newspapermen who arrived in person to seek interviews with Sabina, and immediately hung up on two others who telephoned. Sabina grew weary of the constant interruptions and left early for an unspecified place where she could "have some peace and quiet," leaving Quincannon to deal with any agency business that might come along (there was none) and wait in mounting frustration.

Shortly before five o'clock a Western Union deliveryman brought an answering wire from Clem Holloway. The preliminary information provided by the Los Angeles detective, taken from his copious files, contained two pieces of information that deepened Quincannon's gloom and raised his ire. Bob Cantwell, that blasted little sneak, had baldly lied to him. Jack Travers was *not* his cousin; Travers had no living relatives. He did have a record of three robbery and burglary arrests, as well as a shooting scrape, but his only conviction had resulted in a two-year, not four-year, prison sentence. Whatever Cantwell's reason for lying about his connection with Travers, it had nothing to do with childhood beatings at the hands of a bullying relative.

He had also apparently lied in his claim that Travers had only recently come to San Francisco from Southern California. According to Holloway's records, Travers had not been seen or otherwise placed in the Los Angeles area since his release from prison; was reputed, in fact, to have shifted his base of operations to northern California. Furthermore, he had had no confederates in any of his past crimes, nor any known alliances with anyone called the Kid or named Zeke.

Who were those two, then, if not one and the same person? And what was their (or his) connection to Travers, Cantwell, and the Wells, Fargo holdup? Was Travers's murderer and Bob Cantwell — again, if they weren't one and the same — still somewhere in the Bay Area or long gone by now? Yes, and just who had possession of the swag? Too many questions, and still not the glimmer of an answer to any of them.

8
SABINA

John surprised her by calling at her rooms after she returned from church on Sunday morning. Immediately after, which meant he'd been waiting and watching nearby for her arrival. He was an impulsive man, to be sure, and ever determined in his quest for her favors, but he seldom bothered her at home or on weekends unless it was on urgent agency business. And his visit today seemed to be personal, though of a more tentative sort than usual.

"If you have no plans," he said, "I thought we might spend the day together. Brunch at the Old Poodle Dog, and afterward a leisurely drive in a buggy I've rented —"

"John, you know how I feel about keeping our business relationship and our private lives separate. Besides, I have a luncheon engagement."

"You have? With whom, may I ask?"

"You may not."

"I don't suppose you'd consider canceling."

"No, I wouldn't. Mr. Levi Strauss wouldn't like it."

It took him a few seconds of suspicious frowning before he realized that she was pulling his leg. "Bah," he said. "If you're seeing a man, he's half Strauss's age and weight and doubtless not nearly as handsome as I am. One of the guests at Sutro's party?"

Sabina was tempted to continue teasing him, but it would have been petty. She sighed. "If you must know, I'm dining with Callie French."

"Ah, your cousin, yes. A delightful lady." He was relieved, though he tried to hide it. "And are you spending the afternoon with her as well?"

"I haven't made up my mind yet."

"Spend it with me instead."

"John . . ."

"Not so much for social as for business reasons," he said. "There's nothing new about Virginia St. Ives in this morning's newspapers. Her body still hasn't been recovered."

"I know. At least three people mentioned the fact to me at church."

"Have you ever been to Sutro Heights in

112

the daytime?"

"Once. Callie and I drove out to view the gardens. Mayor Sutro allows visitors, you know, for a nominal fee."

"Leave it to the rich to take advantage of the poor."

"He is not taking advantage of anyone. The fee is merely a dime per visitor for the upkeep of the grounds."

"I've never been there," John said, "and I'd like to see that overlook and the parapet where the girl jumped. Wouldn't you like a look at the spot yourself, in daylight and clear weather?"

"As a matter of fact, I would."

"Then I suggest we meet after your luncheon and take a ride to the beach. Agreed?"

Sabina considered, but only briefly. It *was* business, after all. And a frustratingly curious business at that.

"Agreed," she said.

On the carriage ride to Sutro Heights, John finally made up his mind to tell her of his adventures on the waterfront and Telegraph Hill the previous evening. She had listened to his tales of derring-do often enough to know when he was leaving out details that didn't reflect well on his prowess as a detective, and his sketchy account of his second encounter with Bob Cantwell indicated it had been more than just "a brief skirmish" — one in which he hadn't fared well, judging from the still-visible marks on his forehead and temple, which he off handedly dismissed as accidental. But she didn't press him.

"Whether Cantwell was involved in the robbery or not, he knows a great deal more than he told me," John was saying as the carriage rattled and clanged along Geary Boulevard. "Such as the identities of the Kid and Zeke, both of whom also have some connection."

"Only one man committed the holdup," Sabina reminded him.

"Aye, but I'll wager Travers wasn't working alone. His murder and the disappearance of the money proves that."

"Cantwell mentioned Zeke, you said. But how did you find out about the Kid?"

John produced a scrap of paper from his billfold and handed it to her, saying that he'd found it in the lining of a coat he presumed to have belonged to Jack Travers. Sabina read the scrawled words: *The Kid, 9:15, Tuesday, usual place.*

"Travers appears to have been little more than a strong-arm bandit," John went on, "and none too bright at that. How would he have found out that Wells, Fargo would have such a large amount of cash on hand that particular day, a fact the company is always careful to keep secret, and the optimum time to strike, unless he was informed or perhaps recruited by an accomplice who possessed that knowledge? Blast me, that's a question I should have thought to ask Cantwell straightaway last night."

"Do you think he could have planned the robbery?"

"It's possible, but not likely. He's neither intelligent enough nor brave enough nor well-placed enough."

"The mysterious Zeke, then? Or the Kid, if he's not Cantwell?"

"One or the other, yes. I thought for a time that Cantwell might be the Kid, but now I have my doubts."

"Could he be a Wells, Fargo employee?" Sabina asked. "The bandit seems to have known that a large amount of cash had just arrived by train, a fact the company would hardly have advertised."

"True," John said. "How Travers and the Kid knew about the special shipment is another part of the puzzle. But no, I don't believe it was an inside job. The company carefully screens the Expressmen who handle large sums of cash for them, and their detectives would have investigated that possibility first thing. If they're satisfied none of their people are involved, so am I."

"But you're convinced Cantwell knows who Zeke is?"

"Oh, yes. He believes it was Zeke who shot Travers, and his terror of the man panicked him into bolting. His guilty knowledge of the crime goes well beyond supplying the Drifter's Alley hideout. When I find him, then I'll know what he knows."

"If you find him," Sabina said. "He may have already left for parts unknown."

"I'm banking he hasn't. He gambled away the hundred dollars I gave him and he wouldn't have had much money left, if any. I've a hunch he intends to, or has already, put the touch on someone for enough cash to set him up in a new location."

"Not Zeke, surely."

"No. The Kid is my guess." John finger-combed his whiskers. "Cantwell is not above blackmail. And he's desperate enough to risk it. He'd want more than a few dollars, too, and it's not likely a large sum could be raised on the weekend. I'll warrant Cantwell is hiding out somewhere, waiting for his lammas money. Track him and the Kid down, and one of them in turn will lead me to Zeke and the stolen money."

"A tall order, John. How do you propose to do your tracking, when you have no idea where Cantwell is hiding or who the Kid is? And in such a short time?"

"I've put out the word. One of my informers will come through."

"And if one doesn't?"

"Then," he vowed, "I'll think of another way."

That statement was typical of her partner, Sabina thought — utter blind faith in his abilities, no matter what the odds. In a lesser man, it would have been over-confident bravado. But John had an uncanny knack for pulling rabbits out of hats. She had seen him do it often enough not to be surprised if he managed it yet again in this case.

For the rest of the ride to Sutro Heights, they were both silent under the spell of the fine day. San Francisco could be wickedly cold and damp while its environs basked under sunny blue skies, but when temperatures rose and the fogbanks receded beyond the horizon, it was a city like none other. On such days as this, most San Franciscans could forget the city's tumultuous past and ignore the thriving underworld in its midst. Even a pair of detectives such as she and John, whose work brought them into contact with that underworld — if only for a little while.

When they turned onto Point Lobos, the Pacific appeared sparkling in the sun below; it was such a clear afternoon that the staggered dark shapes of the Farallon Islands stood out clearly on the horizon. The still-skeletal shapes of the Cliff House and Sutro Baths rose along the rocky shore. Construction of both was expected to be completed sometime next year, and their openings would be sure to draw large and enthusiastic crowds. Perhaps she and Callie would attend, if her work permitted it.

One of Adolph Sutro's employees was stationed in front of the high wooden arch where recumbent stone lions guarded the carriageway's perimeter. He accepted the two dimes John handed him, then asked if they were carrying picnic hampers or other such containers of food and drink. Scowling, John told him no and he passed them through.

"No picnic hampers? Bah."

"Picnics aren't allowed," Sabina said. "The mayor insists the grounds be kept in pristine condition, and rightly so."

They clattered along the carriageway toward the ornate, many-domed house, which looked uglier by daylight than it had the night before. Close around it carpetlike beds of flowers bloomed in lush purples, reds, and yellows. The rolling greensward with its scattering of statues that Sabina had stumbled across in pursuit of Virginia St. Ives stretched out on the near side. Quite a few visitors were strolling through the gardens and on the cinder path that led out to the raised overlook. More than the usual number, Sabina guessed, drawn by Friday night's strange and well-publicized events.

As they neared the turning circle ringed by parked buggies and other conveyances, John said suddenly, "What in God's name is that?"

Sabina looked where he was pointing. It was at a large and wicked-looking stone statue peeping out of a rhododendron bush — evil little eyes, sharp teeth, and the suggestion of a two-pronged tail.

"Offhand, I'd say it's a devil. Or possibly Satan himself."

"What sort of man places a statue like that in his garden?"

"Perhaps one who wishes to warn of the temptations of evil."

"Then why does he have it hidden in the shrubbery?"

"The bush may have grown around it."

"Then he should have his gardeners trim

the branches. If I owned property with Satan sitting on it, I'd want the damned thing in plain sight where I could keep track of it."

That remark, too, was typical of her partner, Sabina thought. For as long as she'd known him, he had confronted his devils face on.

He parked the rented carriage in line with the others and helped her step down. For a little time he stood looking at the house, then out at the near-side gardens. "It was across there," he said, motioning, "that you pursued the St. Ives girl?"

"Yes. Toward that line of trees bordering the seaward path."

"Suppose we retrace the course you and she took."

Sabina led the way through the gardens to the cypress trees, onto the path past the ornate French gazebo. John cast a narrow-eyed look at the structure. His grimace made plain what he thought of Adolph Sutro's eccentric taste in statuary and other garden ornaments.

When they reached the stone stairs to the overlook, he asked, "How far ahead of you was Virginia at this point?"

"Thirty yards or so. About the same distance that separated us when she jumped

120

from the parapet."

John took her arm as they climbed up, a gentlemanly gesture except for the fact that it allowed him to press in close to her. She permitted the contact, but moved just enough away so that a gap remained between his hip and hers. Several people were on the overlook, some at the parapet examining the statuary, others on the observation platform looking out at the sun-dappled ocean, still others exclaiming over the glass-encased photographs in the gallery. The sea breeze was on the chilly side, just strong enough for Sabina to put up a hand to make sure the valuable Charles Horner hatpin fastening her bonnet remained in place.

A little more than halfway across the flagstone floor, she stopped. "This is about where I was when I first saw her."

"And she was where, exactly?"

"Straight ahead. No, at a slight angle to the left, between those two statues there."

"More statues. At least these aren't devils and animals."

"Grecian goddesses," Sabina said. "Athena and Persephone, I believe."

"With all their clothes on, unfortunately."

No one stood at the parapet between the two statues. She and John moved ahead to occupy the space. He leaned forward with his hands on the stones and she did the same. This was the spot where Virginia had jumped; the matted down trail through the ice plant was still visible below.

John scrutinized that, then the narrow strip of ground that ran between the wall and the cliff's edge. Stunted cypress grew on it to the left and to the right. The rest was packed earth and stones and tufts of grass.

"Wide enough and flat enough to walk on," he observed.

"You're not thinking of going down there?"

"And why not? I may not look it, but I'm a nimble gent. And I have no fear of heights."

"It's still dangerous."

"Not as dangerous as it would be on a foggy night."

"Virginia wasn't down there when she jumped."

He winked at her, and before she could protest he hopped up onto the parapet, caught hold of the nearest statue, and used it to help lower himself to the ground below. He may have been nimble and fearless, but it made her nervous watching him prowl back and forth along the wall, bent over and peering at the grassy earth.

"John, for heaven's sake, be careful!"

"Always, my dear. Never fear."

One of the visitors saw him down there and called out a warning that he ignored. Others, drawn by the call, came to stand at the wall and exclaim at what one man called "a damn fool stunt." Sabina had to agree with that, and with their urgings for him to climb back up to safety, which he also ignored.

He was at the stunted cypress to the left now, poking among its limbs. Then something caught his eye, for he eased down onto one knee. Sabina caught a glimpse of what he picked up — a small shiny object that glinted in the sunlight. He clasped it into his palm, straightened, and to her relief finally lifted himself back onto the wall and jumped down beside her.

He led her away from the indignant group that had gathered at the parapet, to a point midway across the overlook, before he showed her what he'd found — a small but heavy piece of metal with a tiny ring soldered onto one end.

"What is it?"

"A fisherman's lead sinker. New, and not scratched or tarnished. It couldn't have been down there very long."

"Dropped out of some visitor's pocket, I

suppose."

"Or lost in some other fashion."

"You're not thinking it has any connection to Virginia St. Ives's suicide?"

"I don't see how it could — at the moment." He slipped the sinker into his pocket. "Tell me again exactly what you saw Friday night."

She told him, in as much detail as her memory would allow.

"You're certain that fluttery sound you heard was the skirts of her gown?" he asked.

"Either the gown, or the wind."

"How distinct were the noises you heard after she jumped?"

"Distinct enough. I didn't imagine her body tumbling through the ice plant and over and down the cliff."

"No, of course you didn't."

As they went on toward the stairs, Sabina asked, "John, can you think of any reasonable explanation for what happened to Virginia's body?"

"No. Well, a glimmering of one, perhaps."

She knew better than to ask him what it was. Her partner never shared his "glimmerings" with her or anyone else until they became certainties or near certainties.

She wished she had a glimmering herself. And yet . . . perhaps she did. The same vague feeling of wrongness, of something she'd seen or not seen, that had bothered her before had nudged her memory again when she was repeating her account to John. Its exact nature continued to elude her now, but she had had that sort of feeling before and each time she had eventually grasped its significance. Sooner or later she would also grasp this one.

9
SABINA

Homer Keeps was waiting for Sabina when she left her rooming house early Monday morning.

She had peeked out through the front window curtains and had seen no sign of lurking reporters, but to be safe — or so she'd thought — she'd exited down the rear stairway as she had on Saturday and started across the yard toward the mid-block carriageway. And the chubby little reporter for the *Evening Bulletin* popped out from behind a poplar tree, startling her, before she was halfway there.

"Good morning, Mrs. Carpenter," he said cheerfully. He doffed his derby as he spoke, revealing his bald head with its thin, brown horseshoe fringe. His broadcloth suit was spotted with cigar ash; some other substance stained his stiff celluloid collar. All in all, an unappetizing sight this early in the day. "And a fine morning it is, or will be when the last of the fog burns off."

"It was until now, and will be when I've seen the last of you."

"Now, now, is that any way to speak to a member of the press? Distinguished member, if I do say so myself."

"Muckraker is more like it."

"Ah, you wound me deeply. Such insults are beneath a comely lady such as yourself — the result of too much time spent with that bibulous, conceited, and disagreeble partner of yours."

"John is *not* bibulous, and hasn't been for some time. You know that as well as I do."

"Perhaps he isn't. Conceited and disagreeable in any case. He even threatened my life once."

"Did he? With just cause, I'm sure. He may even threaten it again after the inflammatory article you wrote on Saturday."

"Inflammatory? I merely told the truth as it was presented to me."

"By Virginia St. Ives's brother, who was not present when his sister leapt from the parapet. I was, and I know what I saw."

"Then you should have no objection to telling it to me." With a flourish, Keeps produced a pen and a notebook from the pocket of his frock coat. "An exclusive interview, in your own words."

"Which you'll misquote and then in your customary fashion distort into an attack on the competence and ethics of the Carpenter and Quincannon agency."

"Once again, you wound me deeply."

"Not deeply enough," Sabina said. "The answer, Mr. Keeps, is no. No interview, now or at any time in the future." She started away toward the rear gate.

Keeps hurried after her. "It would be in your best interest to change your mind, Mrs. Carpenter. Silence on your part will only strengthen the case against you if Joseph St. Ives follows through on his threat."

"What are you talking about? What threat?"

"Why, hadn't you heard? He is contemplating a civil suit against you for negligence if his daughter is proven to have committed suicide."

Sabina stopped again, abruptly. The little reporter was smiling eagerly, all but rubbing his fat hands together. "Who told you that?" she demanded. "Joseph St. Ives is in Sacramento —"

"Ah, no, he isn't. He returned to the city yesterday."

"How do you know all this?"

"I have my sources," Keeps said slyly. "Well? Under the circumstances, don't you

128

think it would be wise to cooperate with an honest member of the press?"

"If I knew one, yes. But my answer to you is still an unqualified no."

Keeps lost his smile and some of his composure. "You'll regret that decision. As you'll see when you read my story in tonight's edition."

Sabina eyed him sharply. "Write anything remotely of a libelous nature, Mr. Keeps, and I won't be the only one facing a potential lawsuit."

"Are you threatening me?"

"No more than you've threatened me."

She hurried ahead to the gate, leaving the reporter to stand sputtering to himself under the poplar tree.

Miss Hillbrand's Academy of Art, on Post Street near Union Square, was a beloved San Francisco institution, having produced two alumna of note — Dolores Weston, a well-known watercolorist, and Eleanor Sand, whose ceramics were highly prized. Still-life, portrait, and landscape painting, as well as sculpting in clay and bronze, were taught to young ladies by Miss Hillbrand and her staff. It was de rigueur for wealthy families to send their daughters, artistically talented or not, to the academy for "aesthetic finishing." One of those families was the DeBretts, one of the daughters Grace, Virginia's St. Ives's best friend.

At eleven o'clock Sabina stood waiting in front of the stone-faced building, her eyes on its wide front door. Fortunately she had had no other pressing business to attend to today; she would have had difficulty focusing on it if she had.

The mystery surrounding Virginia's disappearance had given her a restless night, and the confrontation with Homer Keeps and the unsettling prospect of a civil suit for negligence by the St. Ives family made her even more determined to get to the bottom of it. For her own peace of mind as well for the reputation and financial security of Carpenter and Quincannon, Professional Detective Services. Puzzles such as this nettled her to the point of distraction. No matter how many times she reviewed Friday night's strange events, she still couldn't quite identify the feeling of wrongness that continued to plague her. If she did . . . no, *when* she did, she was certain it would explain, or at least partially explain, what she'd witnessed. Meanwhile, she was not about to sit back and wait passively for her memory to dislodge it. That was why she was here at Miss Hillbrand's Academy, waiting for Grace DeBrett to emerge. The more she knew about the post-deb and her various activities, the better equipped she would be to ferret out the truth.

It had been Callie, at yesterday's luncheon, who had told her about Grace De-Brett's art lessons. No one of her acquaintance knew the city's social upper class more intimately than her cousin, and Callie "had it on good authority" — she always had information on good authority, although she refused to say exactly whose authority it was — that the young woman was given painting lessons at Miss Hillbrand's from nine until eleven on Monday mornings. According to Callie, Grace was not only an unattractive girl but a rather dim-witted one, and overprotected by her mother as a result. This was evidently why Sabina had not been allowed to talk to the girl on Saturday. "It would be just like Mathilda DeBrett to shield her precious daughter from anything that hints of scandal," Callie had said. "All that flapdoodle in the newspapers about you, no doubt. But Mathilda doesn't accompany Grace to Miss Hillbrand's, so she won't be there to prevent you from talking to the girl."

Callie was a caution. She professed to know something about nearly everyone in this city, a claim Sabina had never disputed. She would make a good detective herself if she set her mind to it, she'd said once, and then audaciously suggested that Sabina hire her on a part-time basis so she could prove it. The thought of Callie working side by side with her and John, and of his fulminating reaction to what she would surely insist on doing to "perk up" the agency offices — lacy curtains on the windows, patterned pillows on the chairs — was wryly amusing. Fortunately, the suggestion had been made in jest. Genuine detective work bewildered and worried her cousin; Callie was forever warning Sabina against its dangers.

Promptly at eleven o'clock a bevy of young women began to emerge from the academy, carrying sketchbooks, portfolios, and examples of their artistic efforts, arranging hats and capes, talking among themselves. Sabina recognized two or three who had attended Mayor Sutro's party on Friday night. Normally their chatter would have been animated and punctuated by laughs and giggles, but today it was subdued. The suicide and the disappearance of the remains of one of their acquaintances was doubtless the cause.

Grace DeBrett, like Virginia St. Ives and others in the current crop of post-debs, had been featured prominently in the society pages since her debut the previous year. Petite, with upswept brown hair, she had unfortunately been gifted by nature with a short neck, buck teeth, and a flattish pug nose. The fact that she and Virginia had been friends despite the contrast between her ugly-duckling looks and the St. Ives girl's patrician beauty, came as no surprise. Many attractive girls chose homely friends in order to set off their own prettiness, and Virginia had been just such a type.

Grace stood apart from the others, not taking part in their good-byes to one another, looking lost and forlorn. She remained in front of the academy until the other girls were gone, then crossed the busy street and entered a tea room called The Creamery. Sabina, following, found the girl seated alone at a small, white wrought-iron table at the rear, head bent forward and propped in one hand.

Smiling, Sabina said, "Excuse me, Miss DeBrett. Would you mind if I joined you?"

Grace blinked up at her. "Oh . . . it's you. Mrs. Carpenter. You were there last Friday night when poor Virginia . . ." The young bud shook her head, unable to finish the sentence, the shake so fervent that one of the white ostrich plumes on her broad-

133

brimmed hat nearly came loose.

"I don't mean to intrude, but I'd like to speak with you —"

"Couldn't you have stopped her from doing such an awful thing? Really, couldn't you?"

"I very much wish I'd been able to. But there simply wasn't enough time."

"Her brother, David, said you were negligent. In the newspapers. Mama said so, too, that's why she told Inge to tell you to go away when you came to our house Saturday morning."

"They're wrong. Truly."

A waitress appeared at the table. Sabina took the opportunity to claim the seat opposite Grace. The girl didn't protest; her attention was on the waitress. She ordered tea with milk and honey, Sabina plain orange pekoe. The shop, with its cozy atmosphere, reminded her of the one near South Park where she'd spent an irritating few minutes with the crackbrain — John's term, which she wasn't completely convinced was appropriate, for the Englishman who called himself Sherlock Holmes — listening to him lecture pompously on the subjects of tea, the superiority of the British Empire, and his perceived deductive genius.

When the waitress departed, Grace sighed,

blinked at Sabina, and resumed speaking as if there had been no interruption. "Inge is our downstairs maid. She's not really fit for the position, she's Swedish or Norwegian, I don't remember which, and her English isn't very good, but she tries and Mama says she's coming along."

"Miss DeBrett . . . or would it be all right if I called you Grace?"

"I suppose so. It's my name, after all. Such a pretty name, but it doesn't fit me at all. I'm not graceful and I'm not pretty. Mama says I am, pretty that is, but I'm not. I'm just — Oh, here's the tea. Do try the scones, they're dreamy here."

Babbling, Sabina thought, to mask her discomfort and her grief. Eating too much, too, for the same reason, judging by the amount of butter, jam, and clotted cream she heaped on to a scone.

"About Virginia. You and she were close friends?"

"Oh, yes, very close. Virgie . . . she . . ." Abruptly the girl's eyes filled with tears. She took a huge bite of the scone, her cheeks puffing out like a chipmunk's, swallowed, and then frowned, and said accusingly, "She didn't like her parents hiring you to watch over her."

"They felt it was necessary for her own good."

"But it wasn't, was it? For her own good?" Abruptly Grace's face scrunched up and two large tears trickled down her cheeks; she dabbed them away with her napkin. "Virgie . . . oh, God, I can't believe she's gone. She was so full of life, so . . . *here.* I miss her terribly already."

"I'm sure you do. Grace, do you have any idea why she would want to do away with herself?"

"None at all. It's just so . . . so unbelievable."

"Did she seem depressed or disturbed recently?"

"No, she was just . . . Virgie."

"And at the party Friday night? I noticed you and she talking not long before she ran out. Did she seem in any way despondent then?"

Grace shook her head again. "She seemed . . . I don't know, kind of nervous and excited. I thought it was because she was going to meet someone outside, on the overlook."

"Oh? Who? Lucas Whiffing?"

"I don't know. She wouldn't tell me. She said I'd find out when I went out there with her."

". . . I'm not sure I understand. When did Virginia ask you to go with her? Friday night?"

"No. A couple of days before."

"Why did she want you there?"

"Well . . . to sort of act as a lookout. So no one would bother her while she was with whomever she was meeting. But then at the party she said she'd changed her mind."

"Did she give you a reason why?"

"No, she merely said she wouldn't need me after all. I guess it was because she'd decided to . . . you know, do what she did."

Sabina stirred her tea, digesting this information. Then she asked, "Did Virginia ever confide in you about her beaux?"

"Sometimes. Well, not everything about them. I think there were some things she kept to herself."

"Such as?"

"Well . . ." A faint blush colored the girl's cheeks. "You know, intimate things."

"Do you think she'd been intimate with one of her beaux?"

The blush deepened to a rose hue. "Of course not! You don't think Virgie wasn't a . . . that she . . . no, not before marriage. Never."

Protesting too much? Sabina wondered. She said, "I'm sure you're right," though she wasn't sure at all. "Did Virginia ever mention Lucas Whiffing?"

"Yes, but not as if he was anyone special. They rode bicycles and flew kites in Golden Gate Park and lunched a few times, that's all. She liked him, she said, but not enough to go against her parents' wishes when they objected. They didn't want her seeing him because he's only a clerk in a sporting goods emporium . . . well, you know that."

"I understand that's where she first met him, in F. W. Ellerby's."

"No, that's not right. She met him through David."

"Did she? How did that come about?"

"I don't know. Virgie never said."

"But she did say definitely that her brother had introduced them?"

"Not introduced them, just that he was somebody her brother knew and that's how she met him."

So Lucas Whiffing had lied. To conceal his relationship, whatever it was, with David St. Ives? If so, why? In any event it confirmed Sabina's suspicions that he was not the charming, trustworthy individual he pretended to be.

She said, "What can you tell me about David?"

"Well . . . I probably shouldn't say anything, but . . ." Grace lowered her voice to a near whisper. "He likes girls, the wrong kind of girls, if you know what I mean. And he gambles. Mama says he's lost thousands of dollars playing poker."

Sabina had already heard about David St. Ives's profligate ways. At yesterday's luncheon, Callie had referred to him as "one of these young men celebrated for doing nothing." He had trust funds from relatives on either side of his family, she'd said, and an indifferent attitude toward business matters that until recently had been tolerated by his father. But his bad habits had become so expensive and well known that Joseph St. Ives threatened to disown him if he didn't cease and desist.

Her cousin was an inveterate gossip and as such an endless fount of information. Grace DeBrett had proved to be a fledgling gossip in her own right, though far less intelligent and circumspect than Callie. Which had made questioning the girl much easier than Sabina had anticipated.

She shifted the conversation back to Virginia by saying, "Tell me about Virginia, Grace, what she was like. Would you say she was secretive?"

"I guess she was. I was her best friend and we shared a lot, but she didn't tell me

139

everything like I told her. Really personal things, I mean. I probably shouldn't be telling you this, either, but her parents weren't getting along — something to do with Mr. St. Ives's political aspirations. Mama told me that. The things about David, too."

"How else would you describe Virginia?"

Grace heaped another scone, swallowed a bite with a sip of her honey-laced tea. "Well, she was . . . changeable. One minute, she'd be off in one direction, next minute off in another. There's a better word for it . . ."

"Capricious?"

"Yes, that's it. You couldn't always tell when she was serious about something and when she wasn't. And she had a . . . a sort of devilish sense of humor."

"How so?"

"Oh, she loved to play clever pranks. When I first heard about what happened on Friday night, I thought she must be playing another one. But it couldn't have been a prank, could it?"

Sabina wondered. There would seem to be little purpose in a bizarre suicide hoax that caused a public scandal and damaged the St. Ives family's stature, and at the moment she couldn't see a way such a trick could have been worked. Still, given Virginia's crafty nature and the fact that her body had not been discovered . . .

"I wish it had been one of her games," Grace was saying. "Then she'd still be alive and we could laugh about it and everything would be the way it was. . . ." Another tear glistened and spilled over.

Sabina sipped her tea while the girl composed herself. At length she asked, "Did she have any other close friends she might have confided in?"

Grace seemed mildly offended by the question. "No. I was her best and closest." But then she paused, nibbled at her lower lip, and said, "Well, there's Miss Kingston."

"Miss Kingston?"

"Arabella Kingston. She's one of the instructors at the academy."

"Why do you suppose Virginia might have confided in her?"

"I don't know, exactly. But she's much older than we are, almost thirty, and very easy to talk to. Virgie liked her, and once went to visit her at her lodgings."

"Did she tell you that?"

Grace nodded. "But she wouldn't say why or what they talked about."

"Where does Miss Kingston reside, do you know?"

"No. Virgie didn't say."

It should be easy enough, Sabina thought,

to find out the woman's address. She asked a few more questions, but there was nothing further of interest to be gotten from Grace DeBrett. She left the girl to finish feeding her sorrow with tea and sweets alone.

At Miss Hillbrand's Academy, she was told by a receptionist that Arabella Kingston had left for the day. "Oh, dear," Sabina said, "and I had so hoped to see her. I've only just arrived in the city and my sister suggested Miss Kingston might be able to help me find employment. They went to school together, you see. Would you mind terribly letting me have her home address?"

This ploy worked with ease. Arabella Kingston resided at 611 Larkin Street.

F. W. Ellerby's showroom was only a short walk from Post Street. But Sabina was denied an immediate conversation with Lucas Whiffing. He was not present in the bicycle and sporting goods emporium. The same clerk she'd spoken to on her previous visit told her she might try the company's Third Street warehouse, though it wasn't likely Mr. Whiffing would be there because he was supposed to be on duty in the showroom today and once again had failed to show up. "Another of his 'illnesses,' no doubt," the clerk said snippily.

Sabina bought a large soft pretzel from a street vendor, a not very nutritious or filling lunch but all she felt like eating. Usually her noontime hunger was considerable — she was blessed to be able to eat anything she chose without gaining an ounce — but recent events had severely curtailed her appetite. While she munched on the pretzel, she considered her next move.

A cab ride to Third Street was a probable waste of time. The Montgomery Block, where the St. Ives Land Management Company's offices were located, was not far from Powell and Market, but she was not quite ready to face Joseph St. Ives, if in fact he could be found in his place of business today; and if young David was like many habitués of the Cocktail Route and the Tenderloin, it would be noon or later before he went to work, if he went at all. As hostile as he'd been toward her on Friday night and in the newspapers, he might not even agree to see her.

Her best chance of obtaining more information, she decided, was a talk with Arabella Kingston. She hailed a hansom and rode it to 611 Larkin Street.

The block was a quiet, attractive one of private residences and small lodging houses set back from the cobbled street. Shade

143

trees, neatly trimmed hedges and other shrubbery, and picket fences of wood and black iron gave each a sense of privacy. A discreet sign next to the front door of 611 proclaimed it to be a residence for single ladies only.

But the visit proved to be another fruitless one: Miss Kingston failed to answer her bell. Sabina rang the one marked with the landlady's card, and by using the same story as at the art academy, learned from a middle-aged, prim-faced woman that Miss Kingston ate her evening meals at neighborhood restaurants between six and seven o'clock and on weeknights invariably returned to her rooms afterward.

The same hansom, which Sabina had asked the driver to hold in waiting, took her back downtown. To the financial district, the Montgomery Block, and the St. Ives Land Management Company.

10
QUINCANNON

Quincannon's wily brain often worked on knotty problems while he was asleep, so that when he awoke he had an answer or a method of obtaining one. Such was the case on Monday morning. Not the Virginia St. Ives conundrum; his glimmering of explanation was still just that. No, what his subconscious had produced was a possible means of locating Bob Cantwell, if none of his network of information sellers had already done the job for him. . . .

None had. No messages had been slipped through the mail slot in his front door during the night. When he stopped off at Carpenter and Quincannon, Professional Detective Services, he found a business card wedged between the door and jamb and pounced on it, only to discover it had nothing to do with Cantwell or the Wells, Fargo holdup. It had been left by a prospective client, a man whose name and professional association he didn't recognize. Barnaby L. Meeker, Western Investment Corporation, with an address on Sansome Street. Written on the back of the card in a small, crabbed hand were the words:

Your services required on bizarre matter. Kindly communicate at your earliest convenience.

BLM.

Bizarre matter, eh? The phrase piqued Quincannon's interest, as did the well-placed address of Western Investment Corporation. If he had not been on the trail of Bob Cantwell and the Wells, Fargo reward, he would have immediately contacted Mr. Barnaby Meeker. As it was, he entered the office and placed the card, message side up, on Sabina's desk blotter, along with a note asking her to contact Meeker and arrange an appointment if she felt the man's troubles warranted their attention.

From the agency, Quincannon proceeded directly to Battery Street and the offices of Hammond Realtors. Hallelujah. Open for business today.

Bob Cantwell's desk, of course, sat unoccupied. But the head of the firm, Jacob Hammond, a bewhiskered gent in his fifties, was a bulky presence behind his. At first Hammond was unwilling to provide what he called "confidential business information," but Quincannon's glib tongue and a promise to steer potential buyers and renters to Hammond Realtors finally persuaded him.

"Mr. Cantwell was only a junior salesman, you understand," he said. The past tense indicated that the lad's unexplained absence had cost him his job, not that this mattered in the slightest to Quincannon or would to Cantwell if he knew. "He had been entrusted with only a few, ah, minor accounts."

"My interest is in those properties that are presently unoccupied. That information is contained in your records, I expect?"

"Yes. There shouldn't be more than half a dozen."

There were five, to be exact, including the house in Drifter's Alley. Of the remaining four, two were private homes, one near the Southern Pacific Railroad yards, the other on the eastern fringe of Chinatown. The others were business establishments: a small brewery on Brannan Street that had ceased operation the previous year, and a building on Tenth Street near Natoma that had belonged to a recently deceased printer and photographer.

Armed with addresses provided by Jacob Hammond, Quincannon quickly took his leave. If he was right that Bob Cantwell was still in the city, there were precious few places where he could be hiding. He had no relatives, according to his employer, and if his manner of living was a proper indication, few friends; and he was not the sort to hole up anywhere outdoors. What better place, then, than one of the vacant properties that had been under his charge at Hammond Realtors? It would mean he had broken into whichever one he might have chosen, for he'd had no access since Friday night to any of the keys in the realty office, but he wasn't above that any more than he was above blackmail.

One of the private homes seemed the most likely prospect, so Quincannon went first to the closest of these — the one on the fringe of Chinatown. It turned out to be a modest, weather-beaten structure tucked between a Chinese laundry and a two-story lodging house. It also turned out to be deserted. The lock on the front door hadn't been breached, nor had any of the shuttered windows, and there was no rear entrance. This was no surprise, considering the amount of pedestrian and carriage traffic in the neighborhood. The location was much too public for a frightened lad like Cantwell.

The ramshackle house near the Southern Pacific yards stood by itself, flanked by a vacant lot on one side and a railroad storage-and-repair facility on the other. Perfect for Cantwell's needs as far as the location went, but vandals had been at the place; all but one of its windows were broken, as was the lock on the front door which stood an inch ajar. The only living things inside were rats, whose scurrying under the floorboards and inside the walls Quincannon could hear when he briefly ventured inside. No other human had set foot in those dusty, barren rooms in months.

The abandoned brewery, a pocked brick structure with a small loading dock on one side, stood inside a fenced, weed-grown yard. The gate in the fence was padlocked, but there was no barbed wire strung across its top to discourage trespassers. Nimbly Quincannon climbed the gate and went to check the front entrance and the double doors that opened onto the loading dock. Secure. As were the boards that had been nailed across windows on two sides.

One more address to be investigated. If that one proved to be as unbreached as the first three . . .

Ah, but it didn't.

The large, nondescript clapboard building on Tenth Street was flanked on its north side by a carpentry shop and on the south side by a pipe yard. Alleyways and tall board fences gave it privacy from its neighbors — an ideal place for a hideout. Quincannon's pulses quickened as he went past the FOR SALE sign in the tiny front yard and up to the front door. The lock appeared not to have been tampered with, and the plate-glass window next to it, bearing the painted words MATTHEW DRENNAN — JOB PRINT-ING, LITHOGRAPHY, PHOTOGRAPHY, was unbroken and solidly anchored in its frame. He went around to the rear, pausing on the way to examine another untouched window. There was a rear entrance, and here was where his hunch finally paid off.

The locked door had been pried open, likely with the thin steel bar that lay on the ground nearby. It wobbled inward a few inches when he eased his shoulder against it.

He drew his Navy Colt and entered by two steps. Darkness lay ahead, muddled with shadow shapes large and small, but a faint distant sheen indicated that a lamp or candle burned somewhere in the bowels of the building. He stood listening. Silence.

The same kind of empty silence that had clogged the house in Drifter's Alley? He couldn't be sure.

The room he was in seemed to be storage space. As cluttered as it apparently was, he was bound to blunder into something if he attempted to cross it in the dark. There was nothing for it, then, but to risk lighting a lucifer. He did so, shielding the flame with his hand.

Most of the clutter, he saw as he advanced, seemed to be photographic equipment: a hooded camera mounted on a tripod, printing frames, lenses, chemicals, a box labeled MR. EASTMAN'S INSTANTANEOUS DRY PLATES. The light sheen, coming from beyond an inner door that stood slightly ajar, brightened perceptibly as he neared the far end. He stopped again to listen, and again heard nothing more than the faint creak of the building's timbers.

He shook out the match, used the faint glow to guide him to the inner door. When he pushed it inward a few inches farther, he could make out another large room dominated by a great looming shape to the left and what appeared to be a glass-fronted office cubicle at its far-right corner. The light came from inside the cubicle, from what he perceived to be a hanging lamp.

There was enough illumination from the lamp so that he was able to slowly follow a clear path toward the office. The looming object was a printing press, one of the old-fashioned single-plate, hand-roller types. A long wooden bench ran along the wall opposite, laden with tools and tins of what were probably chemicals and ink. He had gone a little more than halfway before he had a clear look through the dusty glass into the office.

Desk, chairs, filing cabinet — and nothing else.

Once more Quincannon paused to listen. The same heavy silence. Faint mingled odors tickled his nostrils then and he sniffed until he identified them as stale beer and greasily cooked meat. He went ahead to where the office door stood open, sidled up to it at a shadowed angle, and poked his head inside.

The desktop was littered with the remnants of at least two meals, a tin beer pail such as taverns and brewers supplied, and a glass that held a residue of foam. He stepped inside and approached the desk. The floor around it was empty except for crumbs and something that gleamed whitish in the lamplight — white with black spots. He bent to retrieve the object, grinned his wolfish grin as he bounced it on his palm.

A single die. One of the pair Bob Cantwell had sat clicking together on Friday night, by Godfrey, accidentally dropped and overlooked before his stay here ended.

Quincannon searched the desk drawers and file cabinets, but found nothing else left by Cantwell. The papers in both had all belonged to the late Matthew Drennan, and their disarray indicated a previous and hasty search, no doubt by Cantwell in a hunt for forgotten money or other valuables. An examination of the beer glass and empty growler revealed that the foam residue in both was long dry; and rodents had already been at the remnants of fried meat sandwiches. Which told him the beer had been drunk and the meals eaten sometime the previous night. Bought by Cantwell with what little money he had left, or supplied by someone else?

He pulled the hanging lamp down and used his handkerchief to lift the hot chimney so he could check the amount of oil left in the fount. Almost none. The light may or may not have been burning for some time, depending on how much oil there'd been when the wick was lit. So there was no telling when Cantwell had left the premises. Did the lighted lantern mean he intended to return, or had he been in such a hurry to quit the place for good that he'd neglected to extinguish it?

Quincannon cursed softly and consulted his stemwinder. It was almost one o'clock now, much of the day having been wasted in his previous searches. If he'd chosen to make this place his first rather than his last stop . . . But there was no purpose in that sort of thinking. What was done was done. For all he knew, he would have found the building empty if he'd come here straight from Battery Street.

A vigil was required as long as there was a chance of Cantwell's return; he had no other way to find the man at present. The prospect of waiting here in this vermin-infested office appealed to him not at all. There was a café across Natoma Street, he recalled — a much better location to wait and watch, assuming its facing windows afforded a clear view. If Cantwell did return, he would surely enter the Drennan property at the front and make his way around to the rear, as Quincannon had done. He had no reason to believe his hiding place had been discovered, or to risk trespassing on any of the surrounding properties in order to climb one of the high board fences.

Quincannon left everything as he'd found

it, even putting the single die back on the floor, then made his way by matchlight to the rear door, which he closed behind him.

The café's front window did in fact command a view of the entire front of Cantwell's hideout, unobstructed except for the occasional passage of a freight wagon, hansom, or other conveyance. He claimed a table and alternated watchful looks through the glass with glances at the menu. Despite the stale greasy odor and rodent nibblings on the sandwich remains, his rumbling stomach demanded food. He hadn't eaten since a light breakfast and his appetite had always been prodigious, the more so when he was on the hunt.

He ordered a dozen oysters on the half shell, a bowl of clam chowder, and a plate of sourdough bread and butter. The oysters were a day old, the chowder watery, and the bread on the stale side, but he ate it all nonetheless. Waste not, want not. Then he filled and lighted his pipe and settled back to wait.

Time passed slowly, as time always did at times like this. He was a man of action, and forced inactivity chafed at him and soured his mood. The substandard food and the cups of bad coffee he poured on top of it soured his stomach as well. By the time the hands on his stemwinder pointed to three thirty, he was uncomfortable enough and restless and frustrated enough to snap and snarl at anyone who looked at him askance.

A newsboy with an armload of evening papers entered the café just then. Quincannon bought a copy of the *Bulletin* from him, to help pass the time and to see if Homer Keeps had had any more scurrilous, if not libelous, remarks to make about himself and Sabina. If he had, Quincannon vowed to pay Keeps a visit and make him eat his derby hat and celluloid collar.

But he hadn't. A follow-up story on the Sutro Heights incident, in fact, bore another reporter's byline and had been consigned to an inner page. There was nothing like a sensational sex-based murder case to crowd all other news off the front page, and just such a case had broken this day.

Boldface headlines told of the arrest by two of Police Chief Crowley's ace detectives of "the Demon of the Belfry" — one Theo Durrant, a twenty-three-year-old student at Cooper Medical College and assistant Sunday School superintendent at the Twenty-first Street Emanuel Baptist Church. Durrant had been charged with the brutal murders of two young women, whose nude and badly mutilated bodies had been found in the church the day before, one stuffed into a cabinet and the other, of a model who had disappeared nine days earlier, laid out as if for ritual burial on a platform in the church belfry.

Grisly stuff, not at all to Quincannon's liking. He quit reading before he finished the main story and tossed the paper aside; contemplation of this monster Durrant's atrocities soured his stomach even more than his meal had. Bloody sex murders were the most heinous of all crimes; he had never been confronted with or called upon to investigate one and never hoped to be. He had no love for Chief Crowley or any of his "ace detectives," but he had to admit that in this case they had done a proper and commendable job in ridding the streets of the so-called Demon of the Belfry.

Another fifteen minutes of waiting and watching for Cantwell, and Quincannon had reached the limit of his endurance. Pacing the crowded sidewalks outside was better, if potentially somewhat riskier, than sitting here on his backside. He could always resume this post after walking off some of his pent-up energy. Or return to the building and continue his vigil there, for as long as he could stand it.

He called for the bill and piled coins on

top of it — the exact amount. The common practice of adding a gratuity offended his thrifty Scots nature, though he did so grudgingly whenever Sabina deigned to dine with him because she believed in rewarding good food and good service. She wouldn't have objected if she had shared this meal with him.

The temperature had dropped by several degrees during the past two and a half hours. Tattered streamers had obscured the sun and were rapidly turning the sky from pale blue to gray. Another foggy night coming up, one more in an unbroken string of more than a week's duration.

Quincannon started up the near sidewalk, walking briskly. He hadn't gone more than fifty yards, into the middle of the block, when he made an abrupt half turn into the doorway of a shoemaker's shop.

His long determined surveillance had finally paid off. The lad weaving his way in and out of pedestrian traffic on the opposite side of the street was Bob Cantwell.

11
SABINA

The Montgomery Block, or Monkey Block as the locals referred to it, was the tallest building at four stories and the most prestigious business address in the city. Built in 1853, it was home to many of San Francisco's prominent attorneys, financiers, judges, engineers, theatrical agents, and business and professional men. With masonry walls more than two feet thick, and heavy iron shutters at every salon, library, and billiard parlor window as protection against fire, it was considered the safest office building on the West Coast.

A uniformed operator in one of the Otis elevators took Sabina up to St. Ives Land Management's suite of offices on the fourth floor. Even the elevator was richly appointed, paneled in rosewood and carpeted in thickly piled blue wool. Sabina checked her appearance in the ornately framed mirror as the cage rose. She looked somewhat pale, she decided, and pinched her cheeks to put some color into them. Not too much; it would be unseemly for a former Pink Rose to come calling on one or both of the St. Ives men looking like that same flower in bloom.

The anteroom in the St. Ives suite was presided over by a young, dark-complexioned male receptionist. On the wall behind him was a large map showing the company's many holdings in the city and the East Bay. Two large oil paintings decorated another wall, the largest of them of Joseph St. Ives, the smaller of his son.

Both men were present, the receptionist told Sabina, but when she admitted that she didn't have an appointment with either man, his manner grew stiff and less courteous. Neither St. Ives senior nor St. Ives junior, he said archly, saw anyone without an appointment.

She took two of her business cards from her handbag and laid them on the desk. "I guarantee they will see me," she said in peremptory tones. "Both of them."

Joseph St. Ives was in a meeting, which was just as well; it was David she wanted to see first. With some reluctance the receptionist took her card away into the inner sanctum.

While she waited, Sabina studied the oil painting of David St. Ives. There was no question that he was handsome, much more so than his heavyset and jowly father, but the artist had captured a hint of the cold arrogance and vanity in his blue-eyed gaze that had caused her to dislike him on their previous meeting.

The receptionist returned presently, to announce in the same stiff voice that Mr. St. Ives had consented to give her a few minutes of his time. "Follow me, please, madam," he said, and conducted her to David's sumptuously decorated private office.

The young man's hostility toward her hadn't abated; that was evident in his expression and his refusal to stand and greet her in a cordial and gentlemanly fashion when she entered. He remained tilted back in an insolent pose behind his desk, and continued his rudeness by not inviting her to be seated. He was nattily dressed in a gray coat with matching waistcoat, dark trousers, and a floppy bow tie, but the sartorial effect was spoiled by his pale, somewhat blotchy face and red-veined eyes. Suffering a hangover from the previous night's revelries, Sabina thought.

He said without preamble, "Have you brought word of my sister?"

"Not yet, I'm afraid."

"Then what are you doing here? You should know by now that you're not welcome." He leaned forward to pluck a greenish cheroot from a desktop box. "If my father has his way, the next time we meet will be in a court of law. Or hadn't you heard that he is contemplating a civil suit?"

"I've heard," Sabina said. "Be that as it may, I intend to learn exactly what happened on Sutro Heights and why before such a suit can be filed."

"You're still investigating? For what purpose? You must be aware of the fact that you're no longer employed by my family."

"For the sake of my reputation, and my partner's, of course."

"And what have you found out so far? Nothing, I'll wager."

"More than you might think."

"But not what happened to her body."

"No, not yet."

"Incompetent as well as negligent."

Sabina swallowed a sharp retort. "I should think you and your father would want to know why Virginia did what she did, as well as the whereabouts of her remains."

David St. Ives said nothing. He rolled the cheroot between his fingers, snipped off the end with a gold cigar cutter, and fired it with a flint lighter.

"The answer may have something to do with Lucas Whiffing," Sabina said. "That is why I'm here, Mr. St. Ives. To ask what you know about him and his relationship with your sister."

"I know nothing whatsoever about that good-for-nothing whelp, except that my father forbade her to see him."

"You've never had any dealings with him?"

"Never laid eyes on the man."

"So you have no idea of how he and your sister met."

"None. Virginia never mentioned it to me."

"According to Lucas Whiffing, they met by happenstance when she stopped into F. W. Ellerby's sporting goods emporium one day. But that has turned out not to be the truth."

"Well? It's not surprising his sort would lie."

"I'd like to know why he lied. And why you've just compounded his lie with one of your own."

The young man scowled. "I have no idea what you're talking about."

"I think you do," Sabina said. "You do know Lucas Whiffing because she met him through your acquaintance with him."

"What? Who told you that?"

"Who told me isn't important."

"The devil it isn't because *he's* the liar, whoever he is."

"The person had no reason to lie."

"Nor have I. A man in my position does not hobnob with a common clerk. Nor invite or allow such an individual to keep company with his sister." He drew angrily on his cheroot, blew a stream of smoke in Sabina's direction. "I don't care to listen to any more of your preposterous notions, Mrs. Carpenter. I'll thank you to leave my office at once. We have nothing more to say to each other."

Sabina complied, returning to the anteroom. There was no doubt in her mind that David St. Ives was as much of a liar as Lucas Whiffing. But why? What was the connection between the two of them and why did David, at least, want it kept secret? It might be because he was afraid of his father finding out he was responsible for the liaison between Virginia and Whiffing, but that didn't explain his relationship with the "common clerk." Or why his eyes had flashed with anger at the mention of Whiffing's name, and why he'd referred to him as "a good-for-nothing whelp."

She waited half an hour for a five-minute

164

audience with Joseph St. Ives, and wished she hadn't by the time she left him. She had thought she might be able to reason with him, convince him to give her time to finish her investigation, if not to cancel his plans for a lawsuit, but her pleas fell on deaf ears. He was too upset over his daughter's evident death, too furious over what he termed Sabina's "criminal negligence." He hurled invective at her in a voice that lashed like a whip. If she had been a weak woman, she might have fled from his wrath in tears. As it was, she bore it stoically and without comment, and left his office with her head held high and her dignity intact.

12
SABINA

It was after two o'clock when she entered the agency offices for the first time that day. John had been there before her, she discovered when she sank wearily into her desk chair. His note and the attached business card on her blotter had not been there on Saturday.

Barnaby L. Meeker, Western Investment Corporation. *Your services required on matter of bizarre nature. Please communicate at your earliest convenience.* Cryptic handwritten words of the sort that would usually have stirred John into an immediate follow-up. He must have been in a hurry to have left her to deal with Mr. Meeker.

She had no desire to consult with a prospective new client, even a prospective new client with an impressive sounding business name and offices on Sansome Street, but neither was there anything more she could accomplish on the Virginia St. Ives investigation this afternoon. She sat for a time, to gather herself, and then once again picked up Barnaby Meeker's card.

Western Investment Corporation was on the city telephone exchange; the number was printed on the card. Sabina placed a call. Barnaby Meeker was evidently a highly placed member of the firm; less than thirty seconds after the call was answered and she gave her name and asked to speak with him, he was on the line.

"I've been waiting to hear from you, Mrs. Carpenter." He sounded harried, as if his day had gone no better than hers. "I left my card before nine this morning."

"My apologies for the delay, Mr. Meeker. My partner and I have both been out of the office and I've only just seen your card."

"Yes, well, I'm glad you called. I would rather not have to consult with another detective agency."

"May I ask why you chose us?"

"All the flap in the newspapers about the incident at Sutro Heights. I believe your version of the events."

"Thank you, but I —"

"They bear a certain similarity to my predicament, you see."

"I'm afraid I don't. A matter of a bizarre nature, your note said?"

"Strange happenings in the fog. Ghostly illusions — the phrase one of the reporters used to describe what you witnessed. The beach near my home has been plagued with such unexplained phenomena and my wife is frankly terrified. I want you to get to the bottom of what is going on."

"Where exactly do you live, Mr. Meeker?"

"Carville-by-the-Sea."

Carville. He now had Sabina's full, undivided attention. "What sort of ghostly illusions?"

"I would rather discuss the details in person, if you don't mind. I would come to your offices, but I have an important meeting at two o'clock. Could you come here immediately? If not, a meeting later this afternoon will do."

The Sansome Street address was only a short distance from the agency. "I'll be there in fifteen minutes," she said.

According to a discreet sign on its door, Western Investment Company dealt in railroad and mining stocks. It was a fairly small operation, with a pair of clerks and three inner doors to private offices occupied by the firm's president and two vice presidents. The fact that Barnaby Meeker's name was one of the latter two confirmed his highly placed position with the company.

Sabina gave her name to one of the clerks and was immediately ushered into Meeker's private office. He turned out to be a short, fidgety man of some forty years, the owner of an abnormally large head perched atop a narrow neck and a slight body. A tangle of curly brown hair made his head seem even larger and more disproportionate. He invited her to sit down, but instead of sitting himself, he lighted a fat and rather odorous cigar without asking her if she minded and then began to pace about restlessly with the aid of a cane topped by a black onyx knob carved in the shape of a bird. The cane was necessary because something was amiss with his right leg that caused a slight limp.

"Yes, Mrs. Carpenter," he began without preamble, as if continuing their telephone conversation after a short pause, "an apparition of unknown origin. I've seen it myself, three times."

"Near your home in Carville-by-the-Sea."

"In a scattering of abandoned cars nearby, that's correct. Floating about inside different ones and then rushing out across the dunes and suddenly disappearing."

"Are you saying that a group of abandoned horse-traction cars are haunted?"

"I don't believe in ghosts," Meeker said,

169

"or at least I didn't until this past week. Now I'm not so sure. After what I've seen with my own eyes, my own eyes, I repeat, I am no longer certain of anything."

"This apparition fled when you chased after it?"

"Both times I saw it, yes. Bounded away across the dune tops and then simply vanished into thin air." Meeker stopped pacing and thumped the ferrule of his cane on the floor for emphasis. "Well, into heavy mist, to be completely accurate."

"What did it look like, exactly?"

"A human shape surrounded by a whitish glow. Never in my life have I seen an eerier sight."

"And it left no footprints behind?"

"No impressions in the sand of any sort. Ghosts, if they do exist, would hardly leave footprints, would they?"

"I suppose not."

"The dune crests were unmarked along the thing's path of flight," he went on, chewing the end of his cigar as he spoke, "and it left no trace in the cars — except, that is, for claw marks on the walls and floors."

Sabina had begun to wonder if Mr. Barnaby Meeker might be more than a little eccentric. John would no doubt refer to him as a rattlepate. And no doubt scoff at his

170

story. She could just hear him saying, "Glowing apparitions, unmarked sand, claw marks on walls and floors . . . balderdash! Confounded claptrap!" And yet, were those fog-shrouded things really any stranger, any more seemingly impossible, than Virginia St. Ives's apparent death leap and the disappearance of her body?

"Have others in Carville seen what you have?" she asked.

"My wife, my daughter, and one of my neighbors. They will vouchsafe everything I have told you."

"The neighbor wouldn't be a member of the Whiffing family, by any chance?"

"No, it wouldn't."

"But you do know the Whiffings?"

"Yes, of course I know them. Fine people, James and his wife — forward-thinking like myself in their selection of Carville-by-the-Sea for their residence. Why do you ask?"

"Their son Lucas was a friend of Virginia St. Ives."

"Was he? Not a close friend, I hope."

"Why do you say that?"

"The lad is too brash for his own good, or that of any young woman who catches his eye."

"That sounds as if you don't approve of him."

"I don't. Ambitions above his station and dubious morals. He made advances to my daughter Patricia last year, before I put a stop to it."

"By confronting him?"

"There would have no point in that. No, I had a stern talk with my daughter. She's an obedient girl — she has had nothing to do with young Whiffing since."

Lucas Whiffing seemed to have a penchant for inciting parental objection in his female relationships, Sabina thought. And with good cause, apparently. Not only was he brash and the possessor of dubious morals, but also a confirmed liar.

"But that has no bearing on the matter at hand," Meeker said, and thumped the floor with his cane as if in dismissal of the subject. "The neighbor who saw the spook lights was E. J. Crabb. He occupies a car not far from the abandoned group where they first appeared."

"At what time of night do these happenings take place?"

"After midnight, in all four instances. Crabb was the only one who spied the thing the first time it appeared."

"When was that?"

"Five nights ago, when the first of the week of heavy fogs rolled in. I happened to awaken on the second night and saw it in one of the cars. I went out alone to investigate, but it fled and vanished before I could reach the cars. Lucretia, my wife, and my daughter and I all saw it on Saturday night and again last night — in one of the cars and then on the dune tops. I examined the cars by lantern light and again in the morning by daylight. The marks on the walls and floor were the only evidence of its presence."

"Claw marks, you said."

Meeker repressed an involuntary shudder. "As if the thing had the talons of a beast."

And evidently the heart of a coward, Sabina thought wryly. Why else would it run away or bound away or whatever it allegedly did? It was humans who were afraid of ghosts, not the converse.

"Just what is it you expect our agency to do, Mr. Meeker?"

"Investigate, of course. Find an explanation for these bizarre occurances, paranormal or not. Put a stop to them before word gets out and curiosity seekers and spiritualists and God knows who else overrun our little community. If that happens, residents will begin leaving, new ones will shy away, and Carville will become a literal ghost town."

Sabina thought he was over-dramatizing the threat, if threat it was, but she said nothing, merely offered a sympathetic nod.

"Carville-by-the-Sea is my home," Meeker went on, "and if such as these ghostly manifestations are not allowed to interfere, one day it will be the home of many other progressive-minded citizens like myself. Businesses, churches — a thriving community. Why, Mayor Sutro himself has expressed the hope of persuading wealthy San Franciscans to buy land there and build grand estates like his own at the Heights."

"A noble aim," Sabina lied. Grand estates built on windswept sand dunes and beach grass? If Adolph Sutro actually believed this, he was guilty of grand folly. More likely, given the mayor's shrewd business acumen, it was merely a ploy to sell the beach land for large profits.

"I am willing to pay five hundred dollars for a satisfactory explanation of these fantastic goings-on. And an additional five hundred for a guarantee that we will never again be plagued by them."

"One thousand dollars?" If John had been present, his ears would have pricked up like a hound's.

"You say that as if you believe I can't afford it," Meeker said, bristling. "Would I offer it if I couldn't?"

"No, naturally not —"

"I suppose you're unsure because of where I reside. It so happens I am a man of considerable means." He thumped his stick on the floor for emphasis. "Our firm specializes in railroad and mining-stock investment, as I'm sure you noticed, and I have a substantial portfolio of my own. I make my home in Carville-by-the-Sea because I have always been fond of the ocean and the solitude of the dunes, and because I share Mayor Sutro's belief in the future of our little community."

"Please, Mr. Meeker. I have no doubts about your financial position or the veracity of what you've told me."

This seemed to mollify the little man. "Well, then? *Will* your agency investigate?"

"Yes." But only because of the tenuous connections between Meeker's problem and her own concerning Virginia St. Ives.

"Excellent. How soon can your partner or one of your male operatives come to Carville? Tonight?"

"You don't wish me to come myself?"

"A woman, chasing after God knows what in the fog?" Meeker seemed shocked at the idea. "No, Mrs. Carpenter. I realize you are a professional detective and your credentials

175

worthy of respect, but after your experience on Sutro Heights . . . well, I am sure you understand."

Sabina suppressed a sigh. She understood all too well. As many advances as she and other members of her sex had made in recent years, most men continued to view them as fair and inferior flowers. Barnaby Meeker was one of them. And there was nothing to be gained, and perhaps an investigation to be lost, by arguing with him.

"Very well," she said. "But there may not be enough time to make arrangements for tonight. It depends on whether or not my partner has other plans and how soon I'm able to contact him. If not tonight, then tomorrow night, if that is satisfactory."

"I suppose it will have to be. The counterman at the coffee saloon on the highway can point the way to our home." Meeker paused. "Tonight or tomorrow night, no further delay?"

"One or the other," Sabina said, "you can rely on it." Even if it meant flying in the face of Barnaby Meeker's objections and going ghost hunting herself.

13
QUINCANNON

Bob Cantwell seemed to be in no hurry as he made his way along the sidewalk toward the late Matthew Drennan's printing and photography building. He was dressed as Quincannon had last seen him, the heavy corduroy coat buttoned tightly around his scrawny frame, one hand thrust deeply into a pocket. In the other hand he carried what appeared to be a small lantern. He walked with his head down and his chin tucked into the coat collar, but even if he had been casting furtive glances to and fro, it wasn't likely he'd have spied Quincannon in the shoemaker's doorway; the number of pedestrians and passing conveyances provided plenty of screening.

Cantwell opened the gate to his hideout and entered the property without hesitation, as if he belonged there. He went straight back to the rear. As soon as he vanished from sight, Quincannon hurried across the cobblestones, dodging a lumber-man's wagon on the way. At the gate he paused for a few seconds, to make sure his quarry had had enough time to light his lantern and enter the building, then pro-ceeded to the rear along the opposite wall from the one Cantwell had followed.

The yard was empty, the door closed. He eased the door open as silently as he could, stepped inside, and quickly shut it behind him. The faint sounds of Cantwell moving about in the office area reached his ears. Flickery light gleamed in the darkness ahead, more of it than there had been earlier: Cantwell had left the inner door open. The hanging lamp would have burned dry by this time, but the lantern he carried must have plenty of oil and a strong wick. There was enough illumination so that Quincannon could make his way slowly across the storage room without risking a collision with any of the clutter of photo-graphic equipment.

He paused at the inner door and peeked around the edge of the jamb. Cantwell was in the office, his back to the window; he had set the lantern on the desk and was leaning close to it to study a paper of some sort that he must have brought with him. Quin-cannon stepped through the doorway, unholstering his Navy as he catfooted past the old printing press. He made no sounds to alert Cantwell to his presence; the lad continued his study without altering position. So stealthy was Quincannon's progress that he was able to walk right up to the open office door.

"Hello, Bob. Remember me?"

Cantwell whirled so suddenly and with such terror misshaping his features that it might have been an exploding bomb rather than four quiet words that came from behind him. His eyes bugged when he recognized Quincannon and saw the pistol in his hand. He made a choked sound and backed up hastily, all of four steps until his shoulders struck the window glass.

"How . . . how did you find . . ."

"It wasn't difficult. You're not half as clever as you think you are."

Cantwell's gaze remained fixed on the Navy. "What do you want? What are you going to do?"

"One question at a time, lad. What do I want? The same as on Friday night at Drake's Rest. What am I going to do? Unless you tell me what I need to know, and don't lie to me again, you'll rue the consequences. If you're still able to do any ruing, that is. I haven't forgotten that head knock

179

and beer-soaking you gave me Friday night."

A sound not unlike a frog's croak came out of Cantwell's throat. His hand spasmed, crinkling the paper clutched in it.

"Planning a trip south, were you?" Quincannon asked him.

". . . What?"

"That paper you were studying. A Southern Pacific train schedule, unless I miss my guess."

Cantwell shook his head. Not in denial, but as if trying to clear it of the cobwebs his fear had woven.

"Los Angeles? A visit to the old neighborhood where you and cousin Jack Travers spent your youth?"

"I . . . I . . ."

"Only he's not your cousin, nor any other relation. Why did you tell me he was?"

"I don't know, I just . . . it seemed . . ."

"The truth has a bad taste in your mouth, eh? Spit it out."

Cantwell said miserably, "I . . . I didn't want you to think I had anything to do with the robbery, that I was forced into supplying the hideout for Travers."

"But you weren't forced. You were paid to do it."

"Yes, but I didn't know what they . . . what he was planning until after the robbery, I swear I didn't."

"You started to say what *they* were planning. Who else was involved? The Kid?"

Cantwell opened his mouth, closed it again, and shook his head.

"Who is he, Bob?"

"I . . . I can't . . ."

"You can and you will. The Kid's name and what part he played in the robbery. Zeke's name and what part he played."

Another head wag. Cantwell shifted his gaze to the window, as if looking for a method of escape.

"Confound it," Quincannon said, "tell me who they are."

"I can't! If I do, he'll . . . he . . ."

"Who? Zeke?"

"No . . ."

"The Kid, then. What will he do, ventilate you as Zeke did Travers? Or was it the Kid who did that job?"

"No. No, it was Zeke."

"And his part in the robbery?"

"He . . . he didn't have any part . . ."

"No? Then who is he? And how did he know where Travers was hiding? Did you tell him?"

"I had to. He said he'd hurt me if I didn't. But I had no idea he was going to shoot Travers, I swear I didn't."

"Where is Zeke now?"

"I don't know."

"You're lying to me again, Bob."

"No . . ."

"Who planned the robbery? The Kid?"

Cantwell gave voice to another croak, this one tapering off into a moan. His face was the color of a grub's hind end. "Please . . ."

"How did he know about the Express shipment and when it would be ripe for plucking?"

"I don't know!"

"Did you tell the Kid about Zeke?"

"I was afraid to, until . . ."

"Until he found Travers dead and thought you might have done it?"

". . . He didn't tell me Travers was dead, I didn't know it until I heard it from you. He just wanted to know who I'd told about the house."

"Does he know where Zeke is?"

Cantwell's head flopped from side to side.

"Or that you sold him out to me for money to fund your gambling habit?"

"I didn't sell him out! I never said anything to you or Mr. Riley about him. I didn't care what happened to Travers. . . ."

"You were afraid of Zeke, and afraid of me — that's why you ran the other night and came here to hole up. But not afraid of

182

the Kid, or you wouldn't have decided to blackmail him —"

"No! It isn't blackmail . . . a loan, that's all, a loan . . ."

"Has he paid you yet?"

No answer.

Quincannon cocked the Navy's hammer with an audible click. "Enough of this pussyfooting. His name — now!"

Cantwell's gaze flicked to the window again. Quincannon saw his eyes widen, his mouth shape an unspoken word; one hand came up to push against the window. And the glass shattered and Cantwell went reeling backward with a strangled cry, blood spurting over the front of his coat. Three more pistol shots created loud rolling echoes; more glass shattered, bullets thudded into wood, and there was the hard thump of Cantwell's body hitting the floorboards.

Quincannon was already on the floor, having thrown himself down sideways at the crack of the first shot. Glass fragments showered his back and buttocks as he crab-crawled to the open doorway. The shooter was beyond the light spill from the still-burning lantern, a shadow shape crouched in darkness alongside the printing press. Quincannon got his right arm up, elbow

183

locked, and fired at the shape, but the cramped position threw his aim off. He heard the bullet spang harmlessly off metal.

The lantern light made him a clear target; he jerked his head back just before the assailant squeezed off twice more. Wood splinters flew from the door frame inches in front of his nose. When he chanced another look, he saw the dark shape running away from the press toward the inner doorway. He loosed another round from his Navy, missed again in the powder-smoked darkness. The miss unleashed an involuntary roar of anger and frustration. He scrambled to his feet and gave chase.

The pound of his footsteps overrode those of the fleeing man's, so that when he reached the doorway, he was forced to pull up rather than go charging through; if the shooter had stopped running and stood waiting in ambush, a headlong rush would be met with a bullet. But the assassin hadn't stopped. There was a crashing sound as he banged into something in the storage room. Whatever it was, it failed to slow him; the hollow pound of his steps resumed. Quincannon swung through the doorway just in time to see the flying tail of a coat disappear through the rear door.

The darkness impeded his own run for

the door. His foot struck against an unseen obstacle, causing him to stumble; he kicked free of whatever it was and remained upright, only to bump into something else. The second obstacle cost him his balance and sent him thumping down onto one knee. The roar that burst out of his throat this time would have done justice to a distressed lion. He lurched upright, staggered to the door.

No ambush awaited him in the yard, either. By the time he determined this and stepped out, the assailant was gone over one of the fences or back out front to mingle with the street crowd. There would have been no hope of catching him even if he knew what the man looked like.

He resisted the urge to go back inside and check on Bob Cantwell. The assassin's first bullet had taken the lad squarely in the chest and he hadn't moved afterward. Dead for sure. And the fusillade of shots had been loud enough to have been heard by passersby. Remain on the premises and he risked arrest on a murder charge.

A wise decision, as it turned out. As he was holstering his revolver and draping the tail of his coat over it before hurrying out along the side of the building, he heard excited voices raised out front. The shots *had* been heard and a concerned citizen had gone to fetch a copper; truncheon in hand, a blue-coated patrolman came hurrying along the sidewalk not five seconds after Quincannon stepped off the property and melded into the flow of pedestrians. No one paid any attention to him as he drifted away unobtrusively in the opposite direction.

The murderer, he thought as he went, was either Zeke or the Kid, most probably the latter. And Cantwell had been expecting him; that was why he had kept glancing through the window. The shooting itself? The Kid might have come to put an end to the blackmail threat by putting an end to Cantwell, and had succumbed to panic when he spied a second man in the office, whether or not he knew who Quincannon was; that would explain why he'd kept on firing until his weapon was empty or near empty. In any event, the why of it was not important. The who of it was.

Only now, with Cantwell dead, he had no definite and immediate method of finding out.

Hell, damn, and blast!

14
SABINA

John had still not returned to the office when the hands on the small gold timepiece pinned to the bodice of her shirtwaist pointed to five o'clock. Sabina considered writing a note informing him of her discussion with Barnaby Meeker and her reasons for accepting the man as a client, but it was too late for John to venture out to Carville-by-the-Sea tonight. Besides, it would require a lengthy explanation, and he would have questions and perhaps objections that would need dealing with. The matter could wait until she saw him tomorrow.

She locked the office and walked to her usual trolley stop a short distance up Market Street. As she waited for the car that would deliver her two blocks from her rooms, she spied an odd-looking individual who seemed to be watching her at a distance with uncommon interest. He had a sweeping handlebar mustache, and wore a stovepipe hat drawn down on his forehead and a gaudy purple satin vest embroidered with what appeared to be orange nasturtiums. When Sabina's gaze met his, he smiled — a smile that she didn't return. As tired as she was, she was in no mood to fend off an unwanted admirer.

It was not long before her car clattered to a stop. She boarded, taking a seat by the window on the right-hand side. Seconds later, someone slipped into the seat beside her even though there were several single seats available. A glance caused her to stiffen: it was the oddly dressed stranger. She turned aside to look out the window. But not before her mind registered the fact that there was something familiar about the man.

"Good evening, dear lady," he said as the car jerked ahead along the rails.

She ignored the greeting. But his clipped, accented voice struck a familiar chord as well.

"Forgive me for approaching you in this fashion, Mrs. Carpenter, but neither you nor your partner were in when I stopped by your office earlier. I was fortunate to arrive at your usual trolley stop just ahead of you."

The use of her name turned Sabina's head. She recognized him then beneath the somewhat outlandish disguise, and was so taken aback she blurted out his name, or rather his assumed name.

"Sherlock Holmes!"

"Zut alors!" he exclaimed, putting a finger to his lips. "Softly, please, and without further mention of who I am."

"Sorry," Sabina said in a lowered voice. "You startled me."

"Yes, of course." He smiled and twirled one corner of his mustache. "Are you surprised to discover that I am still in San Francisco?"

"No, John finally told me you came to see him. Why haven't you returned to England?"

"Ah, therein lies a tale. But I have neither the time nor the inclination to tell it just now. Suffice it to say that I have chosen to remain officially deceased awhile longer in order to conduct certain investigations in your city."

Officially deceased. When she and John had encountered this evident imposter during the bughouse affair the previous year, he claimed to have survived the Reichenbach Falls incident and for unexplained reasons to have made his way from Europe to San Francisco. He might be a crackbrain as John called him, but he was nonetheless intelligent, crafty, and almost as astonishingly adept at detective work as his namesake.

Disguises were one of his affectations, as they were with the genuine Holmes. During the bughouse affair, he had annoyed John by showing up for an appointment posing as a derelict seaman. "I suppose your investigations are the reason for the mustache and the way you're dressed," Sabina said.

"Indeed. A necessary subterfuge for the evening's work ahead." He studied her for a long moment. "I perceive you have been quite busy yourself today. With a young lady in a tea shop that dispenses a rather ordinary orange pekoe blend and scones with blackberry jam, a gentleman with a preference for cigars imported from Cameroon, and a ride in a hansom cab whose passenger seat was torn and exuding its horsehair stuffing. But I do hope you enjoyed the soft pretzel that served as your midday meal."

". . . How do you know all that?"

"Elementary, my good woman. Plain as a pikestaff when one has keen powers of observation and a trained sense of smell. The faintest residue of tobacco smoke in your clothing, a strand of horsehair of the sort used in the manufacture of carriage seats in this country, a fleck of sea salt caught on the sleeve of your coat. As for the tea shop and its wares —"

"Never mind. I'm sure you didn't come to regale me with your prowess, Mr. Holmes. Just what is it you want?"

He glanced around — no one was paying any attention to them — and then whispered conspiratorially, "I have information that you and your partner will both find beneficial. I prefer imparting it to you — you are, shall we say, more tolerant and less impetuous."

Well, that was true enough. "What sort of information?"

"Regarding his investigation into the Wells, Fargo robbery and yours into the sensational events on Sutro Heights."

"How do you know about John's investigation?"

"By the same scientific method I employ in all my inquiries, naturally. The gathering of observed details and other data from which I deduce a sound and if I may say so invariably correct theory."

In other words, Sabina thought wryly, by putting two and two together. But the only way to deal with the Englishman and his boundless ego was to humor him. "And you've found out something beneficial to

John in your, ah, travels?" she asked.

"Precisely. To him, and to you."

"What do you want in return for this information?"

"Why, nothing at all, dear lady, except the privilege of assisting fellow private inquiry agents. As I've said, I have investigations of my own that demand my immediate attention."

"Which I'm sure you'll bring to a successful resolution. Just what is it you have to tell me?"

"That there is a connection between your inquiries and your partner's," the Englishman said. "A connection that bears a central figure — one David St. Ives."

Sabina frowned. "In what way?"

"Specifically, Mr. St. Ives's penchant for nocturnal visits to Tenderloin gambling parlors and bordellos."

"I already know about that."

"Ah, yes, but do you know that until recently, the lad often shared these adventures with a small entourage? Gay blades of similar tastes but far-more-meager financial means?"

"Are you saying he paid for their debauches as well as his own?"

"When in his cups, as you Americans so quaintly put it, he would often do so, yes."

"Would Lucas Whiffing be one of those other blades?"

"Do you suppose he is?"

"I don't know. Is he?"

Holmes assumed his enigmatic expression, the one that had driven John and herself to distraction on more than one occasion during the bughouse affair. "Perhaps."

"And the others? Who are they?"

"I suggest your partner consult with the owners and employees of the House of Chance, the Purple Palace, and Madame Fifi's Maison of Parisian Delights. I assure you he will find the discussions most enlightening. As will you in your turn."

"Is David St. Ives somehow involved in the Wells, Fargo robbery? Is that what you're inferring?"

The secretive smile, nothing more.

"Or Lucas Whiffing? Or both of them?"

The trolley rattled to a halt at an uphill intersection. Holmes glanced out the window. "Ah, this is my stop. I must make haste. I've much to do on this night."

Sabina quickly put a hand on his arm as he started to rise. "If you know so much about our business, why can't you save us the trouble by telling me now?"

"Tut, tut. I am always willing to offer a bit

of aid to my compatriots, but I wouldn't think of interfering in cases in which I am not directly involved."

"Wait —"

"*Bonne chasse,* my dear Mrs. Carpenter," he said, and winked, and hurried out just before the doors swung shut and the car resumed its clattering climb.

Sabina sat quietly fuming, wishing she had given in to the urge to slap the sly smugness off the poseur's face. Should she credit what he'd told her? Yes, she thought. Daft as the man was and as infuriating as he could be, he had an uncanny knack for ferreting out and assembling information that proved to be valid. If it was in this case, then it explained the connection between David St. Ives and Lucas Whiffing, and possibly a great deal more. It might even provide John with a key to unlock the mystery of the missing Wells, Fargo money and bring him his lusted-after reward. Though if it did, he would not be pleased to find himself once more in the debt of the bogus Mr. Holmes.

15
SABINA

After freshening up and feeding both herself and Adam a light supper, Sabina ventured out again. The evening was once more gray and chilly with scudding fog, but she could still smell the sweet scent of apple blossoms that whitened the tree in the adjoining yard.

Springtime again — a season that had once enchanted her. But no more. Now the coming of spring was a reminder that another year had gone by without Stephen. The fresh smells of growing things had the power to strip her emotions bare, and she had to lie to herself that the moisture that sometimes came into her eyes, as it did now, was caused by allergies, not lingering grief.

With her handkerchief she dabbed her eyes dry and sternly took herself in hand. She had work to do, and work was what had enabled her to survive her loss and continue her life alone.

A hansom cab was just letting off a couple

who lived in the neighborhood and whom Sabina knew slightly. She hurried up, gesturing for the driver to wait, exchanged brief pleasantries with the couple, and then stepped aboard and gave the driver Arabella Kingston's address.

Daylight was waning, and lamps glowed behind house windows on either side of the block, when they arrived at Larkin Street. A large Concord carriage was parked in front of number 631, so the cab drew up a short distance behind it. Sabina alighted, paid the driver, then stood for a moment in the shadow of a large elm tree to adjust her clothing as the horse clopped away. The front parlor of Arabella Kingston's lodging house was lighted, and there was illumination in one of the second-floor windows. Miss Kingston's room?

She was about to start in that direction when the sound of hurrying footsteps, two sets of them, reached her ears. A pair of figures, she saw then, were coming up the sidewalk to her right, just passing under one of the electric streetlights. The one in front, a woman in coat and full skirt, clutched a large handbag and darted looks back over her shoulder. The man behind her wore dark clothing and a cloth cap pulled down low over his forehead. Rapidly he closed the distance between them, caught up to the woman and took hold of her arm, stopping her and then pulling her toward him.

A frightened cry ripped from her throat. The assailant clapped a hand over her mouth to choke it off, then dragged her kicking and squirming into a clump of rhododendrons that shielded the darkened front of another in the row of houses.

Sabina was already running by then, sliding a hand inside her own bag as she went. The sounds of the struggle guided her to where she could see them in the shrubbery, the man — purse-snatcher, footpad — ripping at the woman's handbag. He yanked it free, and in the next few seconds would surely have released his victim, struck her to keep her from screaming an alarm, and then fled into the night if Sabina hadn't intervened.

"Let go of her and stand where you are!" she shouted.

The footpad swung toward her. Sabina couldn't see his face clearly, but the crouching of his body and the fact that he continued to hold the flailing woman and the handbag told her he wasn't afraid of being thwarted by the presence of another woman. He took a menacing step toward her, growling something under his breath. And then stopped so suddenly he might have encountered a plate of invisible glass, the growl turning into a startled grunt. The reason being that he was looking directly into the muzzle of the pearl-handled derringer Sabina had taken from her bag.

"Do as you were told. Let the woman go."

"You won't shoot, lady. . . ."

"Won't I? I've shot bigger men than you, and slept like a baby afterward." She took a step closer, cocking the weapon with an audible click. "Release her — now!"

The footpad didn't hesitate any longer. He released the woman, who moved quickly away from him and over next to Sabina. There was enough light for Sabina to tell at a glance that she was young and dark-haired beneath a feathered hat that had come unpinned and hung awry.

"Now set her bag on the ground."

He did that, quickly.

In other circumstances Sabina might have held the scruff at gunpoint until a policeman could be summoned. But doing that might require a trip to the nearest police station to file a report, thus forcing a postponement of her planned interview with Arabella Kingston. And purse-snatchers of his ilk were common menaces in the city, so plentiful that when arrested for a crime that failed to include bodily harm, they were seldom held for long in the city's overcrowded jail; if she turned this one in, he would be back plying his trade on the streets within twenty-four hours.

"What . . . what you gonna do, lady?"

"Stand and watch you run away like the cur you are," she said. "If you've a brain in your head, you'll never show yourself in this neighborhood again."

"I won't, I swear I won't!"

"Then run. Run!"

He ran, stumbling and staggering and not looking back, until his footfalls faded and the darkness swallowed him.

Sabina returned the derringer to its nesting place. "Are you all right?" she asked the woman.

"Yes, thanks to you." The woman seemed shaken, but not as badly so as some might have been. She bent to retrieve her bag, and when she straightened a visible shiver passed through her — aftermath of the shock she'd received. But that was the only sign of distress. "I . . . I don't know what he might have done if you hadn't come along."

"Fortunately I did. Do you live nearby?"

"Yes, just three doors up the street."

"Number 631?"

"That's right."

"Your name wouldn't be Arabella Kingston, would it?"

"Why . . . why, yes, it is. How did you know?"

Sabina smiled. Her arrival in time to prevent the purse-snatching had been fortuitous indeed.

Miss Kingston's second-floor flat was cozy and neat as a pin. Framed watercolor paintings gave it color and cheeriness — cityscapes and seascapes, flowers and trees, one of the Golden Gate Park lakes, and a recognizable scene from the California Midwinter International Exposition of the previous year. All were very good, and when Sabina commented on the fact, Miss Kingston admitted that they were hers.

"Thank you, but they're really not, I'm afraid," she said.

"On the contrary. They have warmth and charm."

"It's good of you to say so, but none of the gallery owners who have seen them . . . well, that's neither here nor there. I'm quite happy teaching at Miss Hillbrand's Academy."

She excused herself to light a small gas stove, then fill a kettle from a pitcher of water and set it atop the stove. Her gratitude for Sabina's rescue had prompted the invitation to have tea in her rooms. She had seemed puzzled when Sabina introduced herself and explained why she had come to Larkin Street tonight; she had read the newspaper accounts of the Sutro Heights tragedy and knew Sabina's name, but couldn't imagine why she would want to talk to her. A few questions about her relationship with Virginia St. Ives, Sabina said, as part of her investigation into the girl's suicide.

While Miss Kingston set out a tea service, Sabina took in the rest of the sitting room. A trio of small tables held what must be beloved artifacts: a pink conch seashell; a small crystal ball on a brass; a pair of agate bookends holding an assortment of slim volumes; and several framed photographs. One of the latter was a portrait of an older couple that had obviously been posed and taken by a professional photographer; another was of what appeared to be a large country house on wooded grounds, with the words "The Gables" neatly penned in to the lower right-hand corner.

Her hostess, bringing the tea service, saw her looking at the photographs. "My parents and their summer home in Burlingame," she said, setting the tray down on a small dinette table.

"It seems quite nice."

"I suppose so, but I never liked going there when I was a child. No other homes on Badger Hill, no one to play with except for the children of occasional guests, nothing much to do except walk in the woods or wade in a stream that runs through them. I don't know why Mother and Father keep it, since they spend very little time there anymore. They're currently in Europe, no doubt having a marvelous time."

"Do they travel often?"

"Oh, yes. Constantly. They close up their San Francisco home for long periods and let the servants go."

"Is that where you grew up, here in the city?"

"Yes, on Rincon Hill. If you're wondering why I live in this flat instead of in the family home, it's because I have an independent nature and prefer smaller quarters." Miss Kingston sighed — a little sadly, Sabina thought, as if there might be another reason why she chose to live here alone, one related to her parents' constant travels. After a moment, she sank into in a deep-cushioned chair and ran a hand over her brow. Shorn of her coat and hat, she had proved to be a plain but by no means homely young woman with lustrous brown hair worn in ringlets. Normally her full cheeks would have good high color, but now she was pale and slightly damp skinned.

"Are you certain you're feeling well?" Sabina asked.

"Yes. It's just that I've never been . . . manhandled like that before."

"No woman should ever have to be," Sabina said.

"No. And for so little reason in my case — I have no more than two dollars in my bag, and never carry any of my jewelry."

"A wise decision."

"In your profession, Mrs. Carpenter, you must have had experience with men like that. You were very brave and very forceful."

"And very angry. Yes, I have. More than I care to think about."

The kettle began to whistle. Miss Kingston stood to fetch it and then to pour tea for both of them. When she was seated again, she said, "Virginia's death . . . it's too horrible for words. I can't imagine why she would have done such a thing. And in such a sensational fashion."

"She gave no indication of being severely depressed?"

"No, none. She seemed quite happy, almost . . . bubbly at times. But then, she could also be secretive and overly dramatic."

"I understand the two of you were close."

"I wouldn't exactly call our relationship close. I suppose Virginia considered me a mentor."

"She confided in you?"

"Not on personal matters, no. She was an aspiring artist, and she wanted to know what an artist's life was like. The pleasant, satisfying, and what she considered glamorous parts — she wasn't interested in the unpleasant aspects, such as adverse criticism. Typical of her age. Girls of eighteen, pampered ones especially, have romanticized notions of life."

"Did she mention any beaux?"

"No. Nor did I ask. She came from a very sheltered background, as I'm sure you know, and I assumed that if she had any suitors, her parents would carefully screen them."

"All except one. Does the name Lucas Whiffing mean anything to you?"

Whiffing's name hadn't been in the newspapers. Miss Kingston shook her head. "Who is he?"

"A young man she was seeing, a friend of her brother's. Do you know David St. Ives?"

"No. I met him once, briefly." And didn't

like him, judging from Miss Kingston's tone.

"Tell me, when did you last speak with Virginia?"

"After her last lesson, a few days before she . . . died. We had tea together, at her request."

"Why did she make the request?"

"Just to talk, she said."

"How did she seem that day?"

"Well . . . now that I think about it, she was somewhat nervous. Not trepidatious. As if she were excited about something."

"Did she give you any idea what it might be?"

"No. She babbled on about art, hers and mine, and about my parents and their home and their travels. Things like that."

"Why did she bring up the subject of your parents?"

"I don't know, really. I'd told her all there was to tell the week before, when she visited me."

"Visited you here?"

"Yes. She asked to see my watercolors and I invited her. She noticed my photographs," Miss Kingston said, gesturing at the table that held them, "and asked about them. She seemed particularly intrigued by the one of the Burlingame house. One of her regrets, she said, was that her parents refused to buy a country home as my family did because they preferred city life."

Sabina asked a few more questions, none of the answers to which were informative. By the time she finished her tea, Miss Kingston seemed drained of speech and showed signs of delayed reaction to her evening's mishap. Sabina rose to leave, saying that she'd taken up enough of her hostess's time.

At the door Miss Kingston said, "I hope you find out what happened to Virginia, Mrs. Carpenter. If you do, I would appreciate knowing. The more I think about it, the more I find it hard to believe that she would do away with herself, dramatically or otherwise."

"Why is that?"

"Self-centered people seldom kill themselves — and quite frankly, Virginia was as self-centered as any girl I've ever known."

16
QUINCANNON

"Thunderation!" Quincannon was so furious he commenced pacing the office in hard strides, the heels of his leather half boots making sharp staccato clicks on the linoleum floor. "Who does that confounded English lunatic think he is, interfering yet again in our business?"

"He thinks he's Sherlock Holmes," Sabina said. "And he wasn't interfering. He offered his information free of charge, as an aid to what he referred to as his fellow detectives."

"Bah. Don't you believe it. He's after something, by Godfrey, and if it's to lay claim to my Wells, Fargo reward, he'll regret it tenfold."

"The reward isn't yours yet, John. Nor will it be unless you recover the stolen money, and after what you've told me happened to Bob Cantwell, that's by no means a certainty."

Quincannon managed to refrain from

glowering at her. She was always so dratted calm and reasonable, as unflappable a woman as he had ever known. It was one of the reasons he admired her, of course, but still. . . .

"I'll find it, never fear," he said a bit lamely.

"Are you going to do as Holmes suggested and consult with the Tenderloin denizens?"

"Yes, and I didn't need the addlepate to reach that conclusion. It's what I intended to do today." This was not quite the truth — in fact, he'd been at somewhat of a loss as to how to proceed — but it wasn't necessary for Sabina to know that.

"Do you think it's possible David St. Ives had something to do with the robbery?"

"The scion of one of the city's wealthy families?"

"A profligate scion known to have lost large sums of money gambling and whose father has threatened to disinherit him unless he mended his ways. Joseph St. Ives may have backed up his threat by curtailing David's access to family funds. If so, and if David couldn't bear to give up gambling and womanizing, it's not inconceivable that he would have resorted to theft. Frankly, I wouldn't put it past him."

"Would you put murder past him?"

"The murder of Bob Cantwell? Are you sure it wasn't the mysterious Zeke who shot him?"

"Sure enough," Quincannon said. "He was too terrified of Zeke, whoever he is, to have attempted to blackmail him. His killer was Jack Travers's partner, likely the one who planned the crime."

"The Kid."

"Yes, the Kid."

"David St. Ives is young enough to have been referred to in that fashion," Sabina pointed out.

"So, for that matter, was Bob Cantwell."

"Yes, and Lucas Whiffing. He could also be the Kid. We have testimony to the fact that there is a connection between Whiffing and David St. Ives. Why not one with Bob Cantwell, too? They're all of an age."

"Cantwell was a small-time gambler, not a high-roller like St. Ives. And Travers was an older man."

"Yes, but Cantwell did some of his gambling at the House of Chance, didn't he? And from your description of Travers, he was only a few years older than the others. Still young enough to have consorted with them."

Quincannon conceded the truth of all this, but it didn't quite dispel his skepticism. "A coincidental link between your investigation and mine still strikes me as improbable," he said.

"It may seem that way given what we currently know," Sabina said. "But there's much both of us have yet to find out — facts that may establish a link, and not such a coincidental one. Holmes was quite certain that such a link exists."

Holmes again. Faugh! Quincannon was loath to give credence to anything the Englishman had to say. The notion that he had uncovered information on his ramblings about the city that had so far eluded not only a legitimate detective but a sane one was galling. And yet, if what he had suggested to Sabina *should* prove to be valid, it might well be the key to locating the missing $35,000 and collecting the reward. There was no gainsaying the necessity to find out.

"There's something else, too," Sabina said, "that I haven't told you about yet."

"Yes? And what would that be?"

"A new client — Barnaby Meeker, the man who left his card with us yesterday morning."

"Investment broker, isn't he?"

"Vice president of Western Investment Corporation."

"Ah, then he's wealthy."

"Moderately, yes. More to the point is his reason for wanting the services of a detective agency — specifically, our agency."

"And that is?"

"Ghosts. Or to be more exact, ghostly manifestations and other eerie happenings in the dead of foggy nights."

Quincannon blinked at her, his mouth slightly open.

"No, John, I haven't gone daft. These manifestations have taken place over the past few days in Carville-by-the-Sea, where Mr. Meeker and his family reside. It's also where Lucas Whiffing and his family reside." She went on to give a brief description of the alleged spook happenings as Meeker had described them to her. "Now do you understand?"

"You believe there is some sort of relationship between these alleged hauntings and what happened on Sutro Heights?"

"It's possible, isn't it? Carville is only a few miles from the mayor's estate, Lucas Whiffing and Virginia St. Ives were more deeply involved than I've been led to believe, and I'm no longer convinced that what I witnessed last Friday night was exactly what it seemed to be. There was a ghostlike quality to those events as well, as I told you."

"Illusion? Trickery?"

"It could very well be."

"Why, if so? And why the spook business in Carville?"

"Those are two more questions still begging answers," Sabina said. "I offered to investigate the latter myself, but Mr. Meeker was adamant that a male detective be given the job. Unfortunately you weren't available by close of business last night, else I'd have asked you to undertake it then."

"You want me to go ghost hunting in Carville tonight, is that it?"

"I have a feeling it's important, John. Will you do it?"

Quincannon didn't much like the idea of spending part or all of a night in the fog-ridden desolation of that eccentric dunes community, but he saw no good reason to refuse. Sabina's instincts were often as finely tuned as his own; the matter might well be important. He said, "I will, yes, unless I uncover information of a more vital and pressing nature during the day. In that case, I'll get word to you and you can arrange for Micah Dolan or one of our other part-time operatives to investigate."

"I'd rather it be you if at all possible. If not, I'm afraid you'll have to make the arrangements with Micah. I won't be here the

212

rest of today."

Quincannon paused in the process of charging his pipe. Sabina had picked up her hat, a gray bonnet trimmed with white lace, and was pinning it to her hair with a gold-and-onyx hatpin. Her outfit today was also gray, a familiar gray serge — her traveling clothes, he realized belatedly. Normally there was nothing about her appearance that escaped his attention, but all they had had to impart to each other this morning had served as a distraction.

"Oh?" he said. "Off on a trip somewhere?"

She smiled faintly. "So you've finally noticed my attire."

"I noticed it when I arrived."

"But forebore comment until now. Eagle-eye John Quincannon."

To cover his mild embarrassment he finished tamping shag into the briar's bowl and lighted it. "You haven't answered my question."

"I'm off," she said, "in pursuit of a hunch."

"What sort of hunch?"

"One concerning what I witnessed, or seemed to witness, on Sutro Heights. I finally recalled what kept nettling me about it."

"And that is?"

Sabina smiled again, a secretive smile this time. "All in good time, John. If my hunch bears fruit."

"Here, now. You're being unduly mysterious."

"No more than you when you have one of your hunches." Sabina finished pinning her hat, took a business card from one corner of her desk, and stood to hand the card to him. At a glance he saw that it was Barnaby Meeker's. "It would be a good idea if you'd drop by Mr. Meeker's office and introduce yourself at some point during the day," she said. "He'll want to meet beforehand the man who is going to lay his ghost for him."

"Ghosts. Bah." But Quincannon slipped the card into his vest pocket.

Sabina gathered her reticule and a small overnight bag that had been hidden behind her desk. "I'll be leaving now."

"Wait a moment and I'll walk down with you."

"Off to the Tenderloin first thing?"

"No. I've another stop to make first."

"To interview David St. Ives?"

Quincannon shook his head. "To interview a lunatic," he said.

The Old Union Hotel was a two-story brick structure that had seen better days, though even when newly built it would have had little to recommend it to the discerning eye. Its lobby was small, dark, stuffy, and dusty. The two old men sitting in chairs across a chessboard had a dusty look as well, as if they had been planted there at about the time the hotel opened for business.

The clerk who held forth behind the counter was somewhat younger, seemed to have been recently swept, and wore a large red bow tie as if to compensate for the fact that he had very little if any chin. He favored Quincannon with a gap-toothed smile and asked how he could be of service, though he was not particularly effusive about it.

"S. Holmes," Quincannon said. "Is he in?"

"Holmes? I don't believe we have a guest by that name, sir."

"Room twelve."

"Twelve? I believe . . . yes, that room is vacant."

"Since when?"

"Since yesterday morning. I checked the gentleman out myself. But his name was Peabody, Aloysius Peabody."

"Englishman. Tall, thin, nose like a hawk's, carries a blackthorn stick and wears a cape and a large cap."

"No . . . Mr. Peabody was tall and thin,

but he didn't look or dress like that. And he wasn't English — he was from Australia. Some place called Canberra."

Quincannon remembered Sabina's description of the crackbrain's latest disguise. "Handlebar mustache, stovepipe hat, loud purple vest embroidered with orange flowers."

"Why . . . yes, that sounds like Mr. Peabody."

Peabody. Bah. "How long was he here?"

"Ten days, I believe. Yes, that's right. Ten days."

"I don't suppose he left a forwarding address."

"I don't think so, but I'll check." And a minute later, "No, I'm sorry, sir, no forwarding address."

"Or said anything about going home to bloody England."

"No, sir. But he wasn't from England. Australia, as I said. Canberra, Australia. Are you sure he's the man you're looking for?"

"All too blasted sure."

Vanished into the ether again, just as he had seven months before. But for how long this time? Quincannon had thought he was rid of the man last fall, but oh no, no such luck. Popped up twice this past week like a damn jack-in-the-box, and would doubtless do so again at some inopportune time in the future. Or opportune time, confound him, if what he had told Sabina on the trolley last night proved valid. That was the most infuriating thing about the dingbat Sherlock. How could a mental defective find out so much about covert criminal activities and be right about so much of it so often?

"It may be," the clerk was saying helpfully, "that your friend decided —"

"He's no friend of mine."

"— that your, ah, acquaintance or business associate decided to take up residence in another hotel —"

"Nor either of those."

"— and that you'll be able to find, uh, whoever he is by —"

"I don't want to find him. I never want to see him again."

"But . . . but you came here looking for him. . . ."

"And a good thing for him that he wasn't here," Quincannon said, and left the clerk looking as if his brain had just been tied in knots.

17
QUINCANNON

The uptown section known as the Tenderloin, an area roughly encompassed by Market Street, Union Square, City Hall, and Van Ness Avenue, was a curious mixture of middle-class residences, medium-quality restaurants and saloons, dance halls and variety-show theaters, the Tivoli Opera House, the luxurious Baldwin Hotel, and in recent years, a proliferation of gambling establishments and sporting houses that catered to the city's gentry. In the latter respect, the Tenderloin was considered a less dangerous, more genteel version of the Barbary Coast. Its name was said to have derived from an oft-quoted comment made in 1879 by a New York City police captain, one Alexander Williams, when he received a transfer to a similar section of that city known as Satan's Circus. Alluding to extortion payments made to police by illicit business owners, he stated to a friend, "I've had nothing but chuck steak for a long time, and now I'm going to get a little of the tenderloin."

Charles Riley's House of Chance, on Post Street, was one of the area's high-toned gambling houses. Not so much externally, the building being a plain wooden one, except at night when the energized gas in a large electric discharge lamp glowed its name for all to see. Inside, it was close to opulent. Fresco and gilt, large paintings of voluptuous women in various stages of undress, ceiling-high mirrors, dazzling lamplight. A well-appointed bar and long rows of mahogany tables, some of them covered now because daytime play was light, the rest presided over by scantily outfitted women, all offering a variety of games of chance — faro, chuck-a-luck, roulette, craps. At the rear was a card room where poker and blackjack were played round the clock. None of the games, so far as Quincannon knew, was rigged. Unlike the proprietors of the Barbary Coast dens, Riley relied on unlucky repeat customers and house percentages for his profits.

The owner could generally be found on the premises, ensconced in his combination office and living quarters above the card room. He was there when Quincannon arrived. While there was little enough trouble in the House of Chance, Riley was a timid little man with a horror of both violence and theft and so employed several security men. One guarded the stairs to his lair at all times; no one was allowed admittance unless Riley granted permission. Quincannon presented his card to the massive individual on duty, waited while it was taken upstairs, and eventually was allowed to climb and enter.

Three items of furniture dominated the office, each so large it made Riley seem even smaller when he occupied it. One was a gleaming mahogany desk, the second a red velvet, pillow-strewn couch that likely doubled as a bed, and a matching over-stuffed chair with flat armrests nearly a foot wide. Whenever Riley sat in the chair, as he was presently doing, he reminded Quincannon of a diminutive potentate on a plush throne. Curled up at his feet was his constant companion, a huge mastiff named Rollo. The dog's amber-colored eyes regarded Quincannon as though he were a cut of tenderloin. As he had on previous visits, he chose to pretend the beast was nonexistent.

Riley was not one to mince words. He said, "Well, Quincannon? What brings you here this time?"

"A few more questions, if you don't mind."

"I've already told you all I know about that fellow Cantwell."

"Except for one thing. Did he do his gambling here alone or in the company of others?"

"I have no idea. I hardly knew him until he came to me with his proposition."

"Don't waste your time with piddlers and pikers, eh? But you do know the high-rollers among your regular customers."

"Of course."

"Would David St. Ives be among them?"

Two vertical lines appeared on Riley's forehead and extended down to bracket his thin nose — his version of a frown. "Why do you ask?"

"Professional interest."

"The same professional interest as in Bob Cantwell?"

Quincannon shrugged. "*Is* St. Ives one of your regular customers, Charles?"

"He is. Or was until recently. A valued one, as matter of fact."

"Meaning he lost more than he won. Lost heavily on occasion, perhaps?"

"Perhaps."

"Until recently, you said. When did he

stop coming in?"

"A few weeks back. Short of funds, I imagine."

Or had his access to ready cash cut off by his father. "What was his gaming preference? Or did he sample all your wares?"

"Dice," Riley said. "Craps, mostly."

"The same as Bob Cantwell, only on a larger scale."

"If you say so."

"Did he come in alone, or in the company of others?"

Riley gave some thought to the question before he answered. "As I recall, he was often in the company of others."

"How many others?"

"Not many. Half a dozen at most."

"Was Bob Cantwell one of them?"

"He might have been. I couldn't say for sure."

"Do you know the names of any of the others?"

"One of the Crocker heirs, the youngest, Jeremy. The rest . . . no."

"Less socially prominent types? Hangers-on?"

"If you mean riffraff, no. I don't allow that sort in my place."

"Not riffraff — presentable young men of lesser means."

"A fair assessment, I suppose."

"Was St. Ives free with his money? By that I mean, did he finance the play of these hangers-on?"

"He may have. A free spender in any event, yes. Must say I was sorry when he and the others stopped coming in."

"Was this man among those others?" Quincannon asked, and described Jack Travers.

Riley shrugged. "If so, I've no memory of him."

"Or this man." Lucas Whiffing, from Sabina's description of the lad.

"That one sounds vaguely familiar. But I can't be sure."

"Does the name Whiffing, Lucas Whiffing, mean anything to you?"

"I can't say it does," Riley said, "because it doesn't." He shifted position in his chair, causing the mastiff to become instantly alert, and consulted a gold turnip watch. "Now if that's all, Quincannon, it's time for my noonday meal. Rollo's, too. He gets grumpy if he's not fed regular."

Quincannon had no more questions to ask and no desire to remain in the presence of a grumpy carnivore the size of a small bear. He wasted no time taking his leave.

A visit to the Purple Palace on Turk Street yielded nothing in the way of confirmation or new information. He had never had any dealings with the proprietor, a man named Kineen, and the employees he questioned were all day workers who had never seen or heard of David St. Ives and his nighttime entourage.

He had better luck at Madame Fifi's Maison of Parisian Delights, which was neither a mansion (just an ordinary two-story, red-lighted house) nor a purveyor of French delights. Madame Fifi's accent was as phony as the name of her sporting house, and judging from the three samples lounging in her parlor, her girls were no more French than she was, or likely to be particularly delightful in the practice of their trade. She quickly shooed them out when she discovered Quincannon was not there for the usual reason.

It was fortunate that David St. Ives and his pals were of a differing opinion and so had selected Madame Fifi's as their favorite from among the dozen or so Tenderloin joy houses. If they had chosen one of the others instead, Quincannon might not have had such an easy time soliciting information. Most of the madams, such as Miss Bessie Hall, "the Queen of O'Farrell Street," were closed-mouthed about their customers. And had Lettie Carew's Fiddle Dee Dee been their choice, Quincannon would not have gotten past the front door — and likely been shot had he tried. After the commotion he'd caused at the Fiddle Dee Dee during the bughouse affair last fall, in the pursuit and capture of one of Lettie's customers, she had sworn to relieve him of a certain portion of his anatomy if ever again he darkened her door.

As it was, it cost him a ten-dollar gold piece to pry open Madam Fifi's sealed lips. She bit the coin with one of two gold incisors, tucked it between a pair of enormous breasts all but spilling out of the bodice of her too-tight silk dress, and settled back on a quilted couch chair the same flaming orange color as her hair. Above her on the wall were two framed mottoes that expressed the sentiments of her house. One said: SATISFACTION GUARANTEED OR MONEY REFUNDED. The other: IF AT FIRST YOU DON'T SUCCEED, TRY, TRY AGAIN.

"*Mais oui,* I know young M'sieu St. Ives," she said then. "A fine young gentleman. Always so pleasant, even when he has had a

tiny bit too much to drink. Never a com-
plaint."

"And not afraid to part with a dollar, eh?"

"No, nevair. He pay for his friends' pleasure as well as his own."

"How many friends?"

"Oh, two, three, sometimes more."

"Do you know their names?"

Madame Fifi lifted one shoulder. "M'sieu
St. Ives, *oui,* because he is so generous. The
others I do not remember. The Maison of
French Delights caters to so many gentlemen."

"But you do remember familiar faces, eh?"

"If they are very familiar."

Quincannon described Lucas Whiffing.
"Was he one of St. Ives's friends?"

"Ah, but yes," Madam Fifi said, nodding.
"A charming young man, very *joie de vivre.*
He comes many times with M'sieu St. Ives
and another young man who is, how shall I
say, more bashful with my girls. Not so
eager or experienced, *n'est-ce pas?*"

"Thin fair-haired fellow with a skimpy
mustache?"

"Ah, *oui.* He and the charming young
man know each other a long time. Once I
hear them say they are friends since their
school days."

Bob Cantwell and Lucas Whiffing, school

226

chums. Well, well. Another of Cantwell's lies exposed: he hadn't moved to San Francisco from the southland or anywhere else. If Whiffing was a San Francisco native, then Cantwell had been one, too.

"It is a pity we have not had the pleasure of their company recently," Madame Fifi was saying. "Or the company of M'sieu St. Ives's other gentlemen friends."

"But he still comes in regularly, eh?"

"*Certainment.* He was our guest again only last night."

"When did he stop bringing his friends?"

"Two, three weeks ago. I ask him why, but he chooses not to confide in Madame Fifi."

Likely because St. Ives's father had cut off his ready access to spending money. It could also be that he hadn't willingly introduced Whiffing to his sister; that Whiffing had begun seeing her on his own initiative, St. Ives hadn't approved when he found out, and there had been a rift between the two as a result. From what Sabina had related of St. Ives's angry comments to her about Whiffing, that was entirely possible.

A description of Jack Travers confirmed that he, too, had been a regular in St. Ives's entourage, but Madame Fifi could recall nothing about him. Nor anything about one or two others who had been occasional

227

members of the group. A big, possibly rough man named Zeke? *Mais non,* M'sieu St. Ives's friends were all refined gentlemen. And names, even if given, were so quickly forgotten.

So the bogus Sherlock had been right after all, Quincannon thought as he departed from the Maison of Parisian Delights. It galled him to have to admit it — and nettled him, too, because he couldn't for the life of him understand how the Englishman managed to gather clandestine information in what must still be a strange city to him, facts that even a detective of Quincannon's talents had difficulty ferreting out. Still, in a case such as this one, he was willing to give the devil his due.

Was it David St. Ives or Lucas Whiffing who had masterminded the robbery? The fact that Whiffing and Cantwell had been school chums tilted the odds in Whiffing's direction. In any event, once Quincannon was certain which of them was the Kid, it was only a matter of a little persuasion — verbal, or if necessary, of the knuckle-dusting variety — to determine the identity and whereabouts of the elusive Zeke and the answers to the other questions about the hold-up and its aftermath. And then the stolen money and the Wells, Fargo reward would be his.

But finding out proved to be no easy task. David St. Ives was not at the offices of the St. Ives Land Management Company, nor was he expected today. He was also absent from the family mansion, and no one there would or could say where he might be found.

Quincannon had somewhat better luck when he turned his attention to Lucas Whiffing. The lad was not at F. W. Ellerby's downtown showroom, but a clerk there told him that it was Whiffing's day for work at the emporium's warehouse on Third Street. Whiffing wasn't there, either, it turned out — he hadn't reported for duty that morning — but this fact was tempered by a discovery that made it even more probable that Whiffing was the Kid he was after.

F. W. Ellerby's warehouse was located half a block from the Wells, Fargo Express office where the robbery had taken place.

It was mid-afternoon when Quincannon stopped in at Western Investment Corporation to introduce himself to Barnaby Meeker. Meeker seemed to like the look of him, which was often the case with clients meeting him for the first time; a detective of his imposing size and demeanor generally inspired confidence.

"I appreciate your willingness to investigate this matter, Mr. Quincannon. Mrs. Carpenter's, too, of course. This ghost business is driving me to distraction. The apparition or whatever it is appeared yet again last night."

"Same time and place, with the same results?"

"Exactly the same," Meeker said. "Only the dune dancing lasted longer this time and was accompanied by the most horrific series of otherworldly moans and shrieks. My wife thinks the noises were made by the wind, but she's prone to skepticism. My daughter Patricia was nearly prostrated with fright. These occurances have to be identified and stopped, sir, with all due haste."

Quincannon said he would be in Carville-by-the-Sea before six o'clock and took his leave. His primary interest was in a possible confrontation with Lucas Whiffing, not in ghosties and ghoulies and things that glowed and danced in the night. But as he made his way to the livery barn on Mission Street to rent a horse and buggy, he found himself wondering if there was not only a connection between the incident on Sutro Heights and the Carville ghost, as Sabina had suggested, but one between those events and Whiffing and the Wells, Fargo robbery as well.

18
SABINA

The hansom clattered its way through a teeming traffic of other cabs, private carriages, baggage drays, and trolley cars, and finally deposited Sabina in front of the Southern Pacific depot at Third and Townsend streets. Carrying her overnight bag, she hurried inside to the ticket window and from there to the southbound platform. She needn't have hurried, however. Her train had just arrived in the station, twenty minutes late, and would not be departing again for another twenty minutes or more.

The delay was not surprising. There had been two daily passenger trains between San Francisco and San Jose since 1864, Sabina had been told, the year the first commuter railroad west of the Mississippi, the San Francisco & San Jose Railroad, had been completed. The Central Pacific had taken over the SF&SJ four years later, and Southern Pacific had bought CP in 1879 and doubled and then tripled the number of daily round trips down the Peninsula. One would have thought that this was more than enough time for the railroad to develop a competent level of comfort and on-time service, but that was not the case. The two previous times Sabina had made a southbound trip, she had suffered delays and a number of other annoyances. This trip was to be no different, it seemed — the third time *not* the charm.

Waiting passengers had already crowded aboard and Sabina was forced to take an aisle seat next to a middle-aged matron who smelled as if she'd bathed in a mixture of lavender water and gin. The woman was not the talkative sort, fortunately. Once the train jerked into motion, she alternately dozed and looked out the window at the passing scenery. Sabina was relieved not to have to fend off idle chitchat; she bought and ate a sandwich and a chocolate bar from a vendor passing through the car, then sat quietly with her thoughts.

She hadn't slept well last night, her active mind going over and over last evening's conversation with Arabella Kingston and what it might portend. The more she considered it, the stronger her hunch had become — strong enough this morning for her to pack her overnight bag and make arrangements with a neighbor to tend to Adam. If she was right in her surmises, this day away from the city would be well spent.

The Peninsula south of San Francisco seemed remote to most people who lived in the city. Small towns strung together between the Bay and the heavily forested Coastal Range — South San Francisco, San Bruno, Millbrae, Burlingame, San Mateo. And Palo Alto, home of the new Leland Stanford Junior University that had been founded three years previously by Leland Stanford Senior, the railroad tycoon and politician, in honor of his son who had died of typhoid fever two months before his sixteenth birthday. A coeducational and nondenominational institution of higher learning for the sons and daughters of the wealthy, such as those in Virginia St. Ives's circle — though Sabina had heard that it had been struggling financially since the senior Stanford's death in 1893.

When the train arrived at the Burlingame station, Sabina was among the first to disembark. The brand-new building impressed her; it was said to be the first edifice in the new Mission Revival style, its roof covered in eighteenth-century tiles from the Mission San Antonio de Padua at Jolon and the Mission Dolores Asistencia at San Mateo. Two hansom cabs stood waiting out front. Sabina asked the driver of the first if he knew where Badger Hill was, and when he said he did, she hired him to take her there.

The cab traveled a few blocks down the California Mission Trail, a six-hundred-mile arterial connecting the former Alta California's twenty-one missions, four presidios, and several pueblos, and stretching all the way from Mission San Diego de Alcala in San Diego to Mission San Francisco Solano in Sonoma. Flanking the packed earth roadway here were a variety of humble homes and businesses — a small hotel, three or four taverns, a dry goods and grocery, a livery stable and blacksmith shop. These soon gave way to open country, and after a quarter mile or so, the driver turned off onto a side road that curled up into low hills grown thickly with pines, redwoods, chestnuts, and bay laurel.

It had been warm down on the flats, but a sharp wind had begun to blow as they climbed. The wind whispered and moaned in the trees, and carried the scents of pine and bay laurel; the latter, resembling tumeric, was almost overpowering. A white-tailed deer, startled by the hansom's passage, vanished in a flash. Here and there driveways indicated habitation, as did occasional glimpses of a roof or a chimney.

Sabina was not comfortable here. A city dweller for all her life, wild places intimidated her — none more than the vast Rocky Mountains surrounding Denver and the isolated wilderness deep in the Owyhee Mountains of Idaho where she'd met John. Strange that this should be: the cities where she'd resided had been filled with danger, and she'd been abroad both night and day on their most perilous streets. Her uneasiness with the natural world was not rational, compared to the threats presented by footpads, pickpockets, confidence tricksters, and the like, but she couldn't seem to banish it. She felt almost relieved when the driver turned onto another road, short and evidently a dead end, and stopped at the foot of an overgrown, vine-tangled driveway.

"Badger Hill, miss," he said.

Sabina looked up the drive. It was rutted and clogged with encroaching vegetation, and most of the plant shoots were new and appeared untrammeled. Six months or more must have passed since Arabella Kingston's parents last came to The Gables. One would think people of their means would have thought to employ a gardening staff, at least

236

on a part-time basis, but evidently not. When they dismissed servants, they must make a clean sweep.

She stepped down and asked the driver to wait for her.

"Don't you want me to take you to the door, miss?"

"No. I would rather surprise my . . . relatives."

"Relatives?" The man's thick eyebrows met in a dark line over his beaky nose. "You sure somebody's here? Doesn't look like any equipage has been over this lane in some time."

"No, but I'm hoping somebody is."

He gestured at her overnight bag, which she'd left on the carriage seat. "Won't you be staying?"

"Possibly not. My surprise may not be a happy one."

"Family troubles, eh? I've got plenty of that myself," he said ruefully. "But miss, I can't afford idle time. Every fare helps me to feed my wife and little ones."

And to buy your daily ration of beer, Sabina thought, but not unkindly. "I'll pay you well for your time."

"Ah. Well, then, in that case . . ."

Sabina took two dollars from her reticule. "There'll be two more after the return trip, as well as your regular fare."

"That's generous of you, miss." In the fading light, the driver's eyes gleamed as he accepted the coins. "Very generous indeed."

"If I'm not back by" — she looked at her timepiece — "by five o'clock, drive up to the house and call for me."

"Five o'clock. Hour and a half, eh?"

"Yes."

"Right, miss."

He seemed honest and trustworthy enough to do as bidden, and not to go rummaging around in her overnight bag in the interim. Not that he would find anything except her night things and toiletries if he did. Her derringer and all else of value was safely tucked inside her reticule. She gave him a nod and a brief smile, turned, drew her cape more tightly around her shoulders, and began making her way up the overgrown and wind-swept lane.

The Kingston summer house, on first sight, seemed impressive: three wings in French chateau style, flanked by trees and fronted by a long reflecting pool around which the carriageway looped. But as she approached, Sabina saw that everything was in poor repair. The pool's water was low, murky, and raddled with weeds; the house's paint was cracked and flaking; tiles were missing from the roof. Off to one side stood the carriage barn, a two-story structure whose upper floor would probably be the servants' quarters. Both buildings had a dark, vaguely desolate appearance in the heavy tree shadows and waning afternoon light. No wonder Arabella Kingston had disliked coming here during her childhood summers.

The buildings and grounds showed no outward signs of recent or present habitation. Sabina went to the front door of the house, paused for a moment to listen. There was no stirring of activity behind the ornately carved mahogany door. A heavy brass knocker in the shape of a lion's head was mounted in the middle of the panel, but she wasn't about to announce her presence by using it. Instead she tried the matching brass door handle. Securely locked.

The wind seemed stronger and colder now, lashing at the surrounding trees; Sabina bent into it, holding her bonnet in place as she moved to her right around the house. Curtains screened all the windows on that side, and when she tried the latches she found that they, too, were tightly fastened. But when she turned the corner at the rear, she discovered a small window whose sash was raised an inch or so.

She raised the sash a few more inches — it slid easily, making no sound — and examined it and the latch. Both bore fresh-looking scratch marks, indicating that the window had been forced. A brief smile touched her mouth. Now she was fairly sure that she hadn't embarked on a wild goose chase.

When the sash had been lifted up as far as it would go, Sabina considered the size of the frame. She would fit through it — just barely. She looked around for something to stand on so she could reach the sill. There was a woodpile next to what appeared to be a shed; she carried an armload of logs to the window, arranged them into steps, and proceeded to climb up. As she straddled the sill, she heard a ripping sound — the side seam of her bodice giving away. Drat! Now her favorite traveling dress had been damaged, perhaps beyond repair. She seemed to be having all sorts of difficulties with clothing lately.

Once inside, Sabina waited until her eyes had become accustomed to the gloom before taking stock of her surroundings. She was in a large kitchen, a handsome black-iron stove holding court over such other modern appurtenances as an oversized oaken icebox, a deep porcelain sink with an attached hand pump, and well-made cabinets and countertops. On one wall was a brick fireplace that looked capable of roasting an entire side of beef.

She crossed the hardwood floor and went through a doorway into a dining room. Tables and chairs and breakfronts were all shrouded in white sheets, resembling misshapen ghosts. A chandelier with many dozens of sparkling teardrops hung above the table, one of the more ostentatious and unattractive ones she had ever seen. She prowled among the ghosts long enough to determine that none of the sheets had been disturbed; thin layers of dust coated them and the floor.

But someone had been in this part of the house recently. Footprints showed plainly in the floor dust.

Sabina followed them through a dining room into the front hall, where a staircase curved upward to the second story and an archway opened into the main parlor. The prints continued into the parlor. Sofas and chairs and tables were likewise covered in there, but one of the sheets had been removed from a large assemblage of ornamental and useless objects — "dustcatchers," as cousin Callie called them.

The adjacent library contained more

ghosts, a fireplace even larger than the one in the kitchen — the wind wailed loudly in the flue, adding to the spectral atmosphere — and more marks in the dust. These led to a row of well-filled bookshelves. Sabina hadn't the time to do much pleasure reading anymore, but she had devoured books as a girl and there were several old friends among the collection on the shelves: Mark Twain's *Tom Sawyer* and *Huckleberry Finn,* a set of works by Charles Dickens, and *King Solomon's Mines,* an exceptionally popular novel by adventure writer and fabulist H. Rider Haggard. There were gaps in a row of novels by Jane Austen and another of Marie Corelli romances. Books recently removed, Sabina thought.

The curving staircase led her to a second-floor gallery. It didn't look as though anyone had been up here; the floor dust seemed undisturbed. Sabina continued her search nonetheless. Six doors opened off the gallery, one into a bathroom with a huge clawfoot tub and the other five into bedrooms. Each of the bedrooms contained more covered furniture, the two largest with ornate four-poster beds; none showed signs of recent occupancy. Why did two people require so much space and so many expensive furnishings in an isolated home that was seldom used? Sabina wondered. The very wealthy were a breed she had never quite understood. It was as if they had so much money they couldn't bear not to spend it.

She was at the top of the stairs, about to descend, when a sudden thumping, scraping noise came from one of the north-side bedrooms. For an instant she froze, then her hand darted into her reticule to close around the derringer's handle. The noise came again, louder. She hurried in that direction, placed the right bedroom by yet another scraping thump, and threw open the door.

Nobody there.

The noise came once more, from behind flowered curtains. She hurried across the room, pulled the curtains wide — and found herself looking at the large, cone-heavy branch of a pine tree that grew close to the house, the wind snapping it against the window glass whenever it gusted.

Wryly, Sabina chided herself for overreacting. She should have known it was the wind. But this remote and half-wild place, with its abandoned feel and its legion of inanimate ghosts, had made her jumpy.

She returned to the stairs and descended. The house was clearly deserted and its only visitor in months had been herself. Was this a wild goose chase after all? She'd been so sure that her hunch was correct. . . .

Outside, the wind continued to blow strong and cold as dusk approached. Soon the hansom driver would appear, and it would be folly not to return to the Burlingame station with him. But there was still time to search the other building on the property.

Sabina fought her way through the wind to the carriage barn, a large structure built in the same style as the house, with dormer windows at the second story. An outside staircase stretched upward along the near side wall. As she neared the barn, at an angle between the staircase and the closed double doors, a slow prickling sensation began to ripple along her back. She stopped abruptly. The prickling continued, a feeling she'd had several times before. John would have called it woman's intuition, but she knew it to be instinct born of professional training and experience. She had learned to trust it, and she trusted what it signified now.

This building, unlike the house, was inhabited.

19
SABINA

For a few more seconds Sabina stood still, her gaze lifted to the dormer windows above. There were three, all covered by dark shades. Nothing moved at any of them, but that didn't mean one of the rooms behind the shades was unoccupied. The windows faced toward the main house; she might well have been observed from the moment of her arrival.

Quickly, the wind covering the sound of her steps, she mounted the staircase. The door at the top was not locked; she opened it and looked into the gloom of a hallway that bisected the upper story. Doors lined the hallway, three on each side, all of them closed. Six rooms, no doubt intended as servants' housing — as if a three-person family on summer vacation needed six servants at their beck and call. And all of them living in close proximity to one another and the animal smells from the barn below, while the Kingstons enjoyed the overabundant luxury of the main house.

The same musty odor that had permeated the house enveloped Sabina as she stepped inside and shut the outer door. She stood for a moment, listening. No sounds here, just the thrashing of the wind outside.

The first door on her right opened into a large single room with a sleeping alcove on one side. The furnishings were few and dust-covered like those in the house. The musty smell was stronger in there: she was the first person to enter this room in a long while.

The room opposite, its blinded windows facing toward the woods and the stream Arabella Kingston had mentioned, was a mirror image of the first in size, furnishings, and dusty emptiness. So were the next two in line. But not the last of those facing the house, with perhaps the best vantage point from its window; that was the one that had been recently occupied.

The room was empty now, but it hadn't been for long. The dust covers had been taken off the plain, functional furniture, and the bed in the alcove wore rumpled sheets and blankets, as if the sleeper had had a restless night. On the largest table was a lantern without its chimney, and the remains of several meals and the groceries that had supplied them — dried fruits, tins of potted meat, crackers. An end table next to a Morris chair held another lantern, this one complete, and half a dozen books that had probably been borrowed from the Kingstons' library; another book — Jane Austen's *Pride and Prejudice* — lay open and facedown, its spine broken, on the chair's arm.

If any further proof was needed that this was where Virginia St. Ives had been since the night she "died," it was confirmed by what Sabina found when she opened the chiffonier. Two carpetbags lay on the bottom, one open and filled with lacy undergarments, and among the half-dozen dresses on hangers was the soiled white gown Virginia had worn to Mayor Sutro's ball.

Why had the girl, as pampered and used to luxury as she was, chosen to hide in this small, cramped space rather than in the main house? Nerves, probably. Sabina could well understand the unease of a city dweller in such an isolated spot as this, especially for a girl of eighteen — and the gloomy, ghostlike confines of the house would have been a frightening place after dark. Virginia must have felt more secure here, where she could observe from a safe height in case anyone came onto the property. Hiding in servants' quarters might also have appealed to her warped sense of adventure and excitement, in the same way the faked suicide and her plans for the future had.

Yes, but where was she now?

She had to have been watching from the window when Sabina arrived, and hurriedly departed while Sabina was inside the main house. Gone to hide somewhere else, of course, most likely somewhere close by. In the woods? Perhaps, but she had no idea how long Sabina intended to stay, and unfamiliar woods were a fearful place at night. If that *was* where she'd gone, it would be difficult if not impossible to find her.

The other possibility was the barn itself. Virginia had been here five days; assuming easy access to the interior, she must have explored it as well as the house and the rest of the property during that time, if only to relieve her boredom.

Sabina exchanged her reticule for the lantern with its chimney intact and several matches lying beside it, though not before transferring the derringer to her coat pocket. Then she hurried back to the outside staircase. In the waning afternoon light, deep shadows had begun to form among the surrounding trees and to march across the deserted driveway and grounds. The wind seemed even colder now, like the sting of nibbling teeth on her face as she descended the stairs.

There was no padlock on the double doors to the barn, nor did it look as if there had ever been one; the Kingstons were either trusting souls or whichever servant assigned the task of attending to the barn had been neglectful. A gap like a skinny mouth yawned between the two halves. Sabina widened the gap and stepped through into a heavy darkness broken only by the fading daylight behind her and thin fingerlings that slanted in here and there through chinks in the wall boards.

The prickling sensation started again as soon as she was inside, stronger than before.

This was where Virginia had come, where she was hiding now.

Sabina paused for a moment to listen. Silence, except for the wind gusts. The air inside was close, thick with odors that clogged her nostrils and forced her to breathe through her mouth — carriage and harness leather, moldy hay, animal and rodent droppings, the faint leftover effluvia of horses. Shapes loomed ahead of and around her, the largest of them a pair of carriages parked on the runway; the rest were unidentifiable in the thick gloom.

She set the lantern down, removed the chimney, then reached behind her to pull the door half closed so she could strike a match and apply it to the wick. When she straightened and held the lantern high, its light revealed some though not all of the cavernous interior. Along the right-hand wall stood a row of three horse stalls, behind which was a closed door that would lead to the corral outside, and above which was a hayloft; a sturdy ladder angled upward to the loft. The other wall had been partitioned off to form what appeared to be a workroom. The parked conveyances were a light spring wagon and a once-elegant Studebaker buggy with its caliche top buttoned up. As she started toward the buggy, the reach of the lantern's light extended far enough beyond for her to make out an enclosure that she took to be a harness room.

The Studebaker bore the monogrammed gold letters RLK on its doors. Sabina opened one door and extended the lantern inside. The interior was empty, and judging from the film of dust on the seats and floor, it had been empty since the rig was stored here.

There was nothing in the bed of the spring

wagon, nothing on or under its seat. Sabina moved from there to the open workroom. It contained nothing more than a hodgepodge of hand tools, gardening implements, and castoff items from both the main house and servants' quarters.

The harness room next. Wary of a possible attack, she opened the door carefully and stood on the threshold instead of entering. Buckles and bit chains gleamed in the narrow space within, and she saw the shapes of bridles and similar gear. Dust was the only thing on the floor.

She went back toward the front, stopped again when something made a scurrying noise among the floor shadows. She lowered the lantern in time to see the tail end of a packrat disappear behind one of the stalls. Rodents didn't frighten her as they did many women, but neither were they tolerable company, particularly in a place like this.

Sabina examined the stalls next, leaning into each with the lantern. If the girl were hiding in a hay pile, it would have to be close to the surface to avoid the risk of suffocation; she poked fingers into each pile in turn, stifling more than one sneeze from the stirred-up dust, and felt nothing but hay. Nor was there any sign of Virginia in the dirt-floored area behind the stalls, just thin scatterings of straw and long-dried droppings.

Dressed as she was, the prospect of climbing up into the hayloft held little appeal even though her traveling dress was already ruined. She ascended anyway, again with caution, holding her skirts up with one hand, the other lifting the lantern above her head. But the loft contained nothing more than a few tightly stacked bales of decaying hay and another scattering of loose straw that wouldn't have concealed the packrat, much less a young woman.

Nor did there seem to be any conceivable hiding places in the barn that she might have overlooked. She searched from one end to the other to make absolutely sure. Virginia had been here, Sabina was certain of that. Could she have slipped out somehow?

No. She couldn't have managed to escape without opening one of the door halves, and if she'd done that, the sudden voice of the wind would have been like the sounding of an alarm. Besides, the rippling between Sabina's shoulder blades was as strong as ever, her trained instincts telling her forcefully that Virginia was still here somewhere.

But *where*?

How could the dratted girl have hidden

herself so completely and cleverly that a skilled detective had been unable to find her?

20
QUINCANNON

Shortly past four thirty, huddled inside his greatcoat, Quincannon drove his hired horse and buggy out past Sutro Heights and the construction sites of Cliff House and Sutro Baths, and onto the Great Highway. Another night of blanketing fog was in the offing. A chill southwesterly wind was blowing in heavy curls and twists from the fogbank anchored offshore; the grayness was already thick enough to hide the ocean from the road, though he could hear the distant murmur of surf and the barking of sea lions. The Potato Patch foghorn gave off its hollow moan at regularly spaced intervals.

This was a relatively bleak, lonesome section of the city, sparsely traveled beyond the mayor's lofty estate. The only structure of note between it and Carville was Dickey's Road House. As he rattled past there and the Ocean Boulevard turning into Golden Gate Park, a long wagon emerged from the junglelike tangle of scrub pine and manzanita that marked the park's western edge and clattered away behind him into the road house yard; otherwise he saw no one. Empty sand-blown roadway, grass-topped dunes, seagulls, fog . . . a virtual wasteland. There were no lampposts here, south of the park. At night, when the fog was heavy and the wind blew strongly, the highway would at times be impassable, even with the most powerful of lanterns, to all but the blind and the foolhardy.

The sea mist alternately thinned and thickened again at intervals until he reached Carville, where it rolled in like a massive gray shroud spread out over the barren dunes. Carville-by-the-Sea. Faugh. Some name for a scattering of weather-rusted streetcars and cobbled-together board shacks that had been turned into habitations of one type or another. Men of means such as Barnaby Meeker and James Whiffing were daft to choose such an isolated and desolate neighborhood as permanent residence for themselves and their families.

San Francisco's transit companies were the culprits. When the city began replacing horse-drawn cars with cable cars and electric streetcars, some obsolete carriages had been sold to individuals for ten dollars if the car had no seats, twenty dollars if it did; the rest were abandoned out here among the dunes, awaiting new buyers or to succumb to rust and rot in the salty sea winds. A gripman for the Ellis Street line had been the first to see the nesting possibilities; the previous year, after purchasing a lot near the terminus of Judah Street, he had joined three old North Beach & Mission horse cars and mounted them on stilts above the shifting sand. The edifice was still standing; Quincannon passed it on the way, a forlorn sight half-obscured by the blowing mist.

Farther south, where the Park and Ocean railway line terminated, a Civil War vet named Colonel Charles Daily made his home in a shell-decorated Realtor's shed. An entrepreneur, Daily had bought three cars and rented them at five dollars each — one to a ladies' bicycle club known as The Falcons — and also opened a coffee saloon. Others, Meeker and Whiffing among them, bought their own cars and had them towed into various configurations in the vicinity. A reporter for the *Bulletin* had dubbed the place Beachside, but residents preferred Carville-by-the-Sea and the general public shortened that to Carville.

Quincannon had been there before, on an outing with a young woman of his acquaintance who had not been averse to spending two rather amorous nights in a car that belonged to one of her relatives. She had since moved to San Jose, but that had been after the end of their brief romance; she had been a mere dalliance for him, as he no doubt had been for her. The only woman he had ever pined for, blast it, was Sabina. Even if the glorious day should come when she succumbed to his blandishments, it would be much more than a dalliance for both of them. Of that much he was certain.

Carville had grown since his last visit. Most of the structures built from the former cars were strung close together east of the highway, a few others spaced widely apart among the seaward dunes. Most seemed to be more or less permanent homes — single or double-stacked cars, some drawn together in horseshoe shapes for protection against the wind, and embellished by lean-tos and fenced porches. A few would be part-time dwellings — clubhouses, weekend retreats, or rendezvous for lovers. The whole had a colorless, windblown, sanded appearance that blue sky and sunlight did little to brighten. On days and evenings like this one, it was downright dismal.

The coffee saloon, a single car with a slant-roofed front portico, bore a painted sign: THE ANNEX. Smoke dribbled out of its chimney, to be snatched away immediately by the wind. Behind it was a corral and carriage barn where some local residents chose to keep their animals and equipage. Quincannon pulled the buggy off the road under the portico, affixed the weighted hitch strap to the horse's bit, and went inside.

It was a rudimentary place, with a narrow foot-railed counter running most of its width. There were no tables or benches or decorations of any kind. The smells of strong-brewed coffee and pitch pine burning in a potbellied stove were welcome after the long, cold ride from downtown.

The counterman was a stooped oldster with white whiskers and tufts of hair that grew patchily from his scalp like saw grass atop the beach dunes. Quincannon sensed from the man's demeanor that he was the garrulous type, hungry for company, and this proved to be the case.

"One coffee coming up," the oldster said, and then as he served it in a steaming mug, "Colder than a witch's titty out there. My name's Potter, but call me Caleb, ever'body does. Passing by or visiting, are ye?"

"John Quincannon. Visiting."

"Ye don't mind me asking who?"

"The Barnaby Meekers."

"Nice folks, Mr. and Mrs. Meeker. Pretty little daughter, too. You a friend of theirs?"

"A business acquaintance of Mr. Meeker." Quincannon sugared his coffee, found it still too potent, and added another spoonful. "How far is their home from here?"

"Not far," Caleb said. "Take the branch lane seaward about fifty yards south, then the first left-hand fork. That'll be Seashell Lane, though it ain't marked as such. Can't miss the Meeker place — biggest collection of cars out that way, and their name's on a sign close by."

"I understand the Whiffing family also lives here."

"That they do. More well-to-do folks helping to put Carville on the map. You know them, too?"

"The son, Lucas," Quincannon lied.

"Ambitious lad," Caleb said. "Sports minded and a mite rascally, but then so was I at his age. How do ye happen to know him?"

"Through mutual acquaintances. One is David St. Ives."

"St. Ives, eh? Related to that girl disappeared off the Heights, isn't he?"

"Her brother. Has he ever come visiting Lucas?"

"Not to my recollection."

"How about Bob Cantwell or Jack Travers?"

"Nope, never heard those names."

Quincannon described the two men. Caleb shook his head at each description; if either or both had been in Carville, he hadn't seen them. "How come you're askin' about these gents?"

"A private matter of no consequence." Quincannon sipped his coffee, then said conversationally, "Strange goings-on out here of late, I'm told."

"How's that? Strange goings-on?"

"Spook lights in unoccupied cars and vanishing shapes in the dunes."

"Oh, that," Caleb said. "Mr. Meeker told ye, I expect."

"He did."

"Well, I ain't one to dispute a man like Barnaby Meeker, nor any other man with two good eyes, but it's a tempest in a teapot, ye ask me."

"You haven't seen these apparitions yourself, then?"

"No, and nobody else has, neither, 'cept the Meekers and a fella name of Crabb, neighbor of theirs out in the dunes." Caleb leaned forward and said confidentially, even though there was no one else in the car,

"Just between you and me and a lamppost, I wouldn't put too much stock in what Mr. E. J. Crabb has to say on the subject."

"Why is that?"

"Well, he's kind of a queer bird. Wouldn't think it to look at him, big strapping fella, but he's scared to death of haunts. Come in here the morning he first seen whatever it was and he was white as a ghost himself. Asked me all sorts of questions about spooks and such, whether we'd had 'em out here before. I told him no and 'twas likely somebody out with a lantern, or his eyes playing tricks in the fog, but he was convinced he seen the ghost two nights in a row." Caleb chuckled, revealing loose-fitting, store-bought teeth. "Some folks sure is gullible."

"He lives alone, does he?" Quincannon asked.

"Yep. Keeps to himself, don't have much truck with any of the rest of us."

"Has he been in Carville long?"

"Five or six months. Squatter, unless I miss my guess. I can spot 'em, the ones just move in all of a sudden and take over a car without paying for the privilege."

"What does he do for a living?"

"He never said and I don't like to pry. But I heard young Whiffing say to his father that

Crabb's a construction worker."

"Lucas knows him, then."

"To pass the time of day with. Seen 'em doing that now and then."

Quincannon finished his coffee, declined a refill, asked and was told where the Whiffings lived, and went out to the rented buggy. The Whiffing residence being the closest, just down the road a ways, he made that his first stop. Four cars drawn together in a square and surrounded by sand, sea grass, and gorse shrubs. Elegant seaside living, he thought sourly.

The stop netted him nothing. The only member of the family at home was Mrs. Whiffing, a thin, birdlike woman. Lucas wasn't expected for another hour or so, she told him. Was he a friend of her son? Quincannon told her the same half truth he'd given Caleb, omitting mention of Cantwell, Travers, and David St. Ives, handed her one of his business cards, and said that he would be staying overnight at the Meekers' home. If Lucas came to see him, well and good. In any event his presence in Carville would give the lad cause for wonder and perhaps consternation.

The branch lane that led to the Meekers' home was easy enough to find even in the heavy mist. The buggy alternately bounced and slogged along the sandy surface; once, a hidden rut lifted Quincannon off the seat and made him pull back hard enough on the reins to nearly jerk the horse's head through the martingale loops. Neither this nor the cold wind nor the bleakness dampened his spirits. A few minor discomforts were a small price to pay when he was closing in, as he felt now that he was, on the finish of an investigation and its attendant remuneration.

The lane led in among the dunes, dipped down into a hollow where it split into two forks. In that direction, Quincannon could see a group of four traction cars, two set end to end, the others at a right and a left angle at the far ends, like an arrangement of dominoes; mist-diffused lamplight showed faintly behind curtained windows in one of the two middle cars. A ways down the left fork stood a single car canted slightly against the dune behind it; some distance beyond it, eight or nine abandoned cars were jumbled together among the sand hills as if tossed there by a giant's hand. Pennants of fog gave them an insubstantial, almost ethereal aspect, one that would be enhanced by darkness and imagination. A ghost's lair, indeed.

He left the buggy at the intersection of

the two lanes, ground-hitched the horse, and trudged through the drifted sand along the right-hand fork. No lights or chimney smoke showed in the single canted car; he bypassed it and continued on to the jumble.

From outside there was nothing about any of the abandoned cars to catch the eye. They were or had been painted in various colors, according to which transit company owned them; half had been there long enough for the colors to fade entirely and the metal and glass surfaces to become sand-pitted. Three had belonged to the Market Street Railway, four to the Ferries and Point Lobos Railway, the remaining two to the California Street Cable Railroad.

Quincannon wound his way among them. No one had prowled here recently; the sand was wind-scoured to a smoothness that bore no footprints or anything other than tufts of saw grass. He trudged back to the nearest one, stepped up and inside. All the seats had been removed; he had a brief and unpleasant feeling of standing inside a giant steel coffin. There was nothing in it other than a dusting of sand that had blown in through the open doorway. And no signs that anyone had been inside since it was discarded.

He investigated a second car, then a third.

These, too, had had their seats removed. Only the second contained anything to take his attention: faint scuff marks in the drifted sand, the fresh clawlike scratches on walls and floor that Barnaby Meeker had told Sabina about. The source and meaning of the scratches defied completely accurate guessing as to their origin.

When he stepped outside, with the intention of entering the next nearest car, a man appeared suddenly from around the end of the car. The newcomer stood glowering with his hands fisted on his hips and his legs spread, and demanded, "Who're you? What you doing here?"

Without replying, Quincannon took his measure. He was some shy of forty, clean-shaven except for a bristly stubble, with thick arms and hips broader than his shoulders. The staring eyes were the size and color of blackberries. The man seemed edgy as well as suspicious. None of this was as arresting as the fact that he wore a holstered revolver, the tail of his coat swept back and his hand on the weapon's gnarled butt — a large-bore Bisley Colt, judging from its size.

"Mister, I asked you who you are and what you're doing here."

"Having a look around. My name's Quincannon. And you, I expect, would be E. J. Crabb."

"How d'you know my name?"

"Barnaby Meeker mentioned it."

"That so? Meeker a friend of yours?"

"Business acquaintance."

"That still don't explain what you're doing poking around these cars."

"I'm thinking of buying some of them," Quincannon lied glibly.

"Why?"

"For the same reason you and the Meekers and the Whiffings bought theirs. You do know the Whiffings?"

"What's that to you?"

"And you did buy your car?"

Crabb's suspicion seemed to have deepened. "Who says I didn't?"

"A question of curiosity, my friend, that's all."

"You're damn curious about everything, ain't you?"

"It's my nature." Quincannon let his gaze rest on the cars for a few seconds. "Ghosts and goblins," he said then, "and things that go bump in the night."

"What?" Crabb jerked as if he'd been struck. The hand hovering above the holstered Bisley shook visibly. "What're you talking about?"

"Why, I understand these cars are haunted. Fascinating, if true."

"It ain't true! No such things as ghosts!"

"It has been my experience that there are," Quincannon said sagely. "Oh, the tales I could tell you of the spirit world and its evil manifestations —"

"I don't want to hear 'em, I don't believe none of it," Crabb said, but it was plain that he did. And that the prospect terrified him as much as Caleb Potter had indicated.

"Mr. Meeker tells me you've seen the apparition that inhabits these cars. Dancing lights, a glowing shape that races across the tops of dunes and then vanishes, poof, without a trace —"

"I ain't gonna talk about that. No, I ain't!"

"I find the subject intriguing myself," Quincannon said. "As a matter of fact, I'm hoping there is a ghost and that it occupies the very car I purchase. I'd welcome the company on a dark winter's night."

Crabb made a noise like the whimper of a hound, turned abruptly, and scurried away to the end of the car. There he stopped, looked over his shoulder, and called out, "You know what's good for you, mister, you stay away from those cars. Stay away!" Then he was gone into the swirling mist.

Quincannon finished his canvass of

the remaining cars. Two others showed faint footprints and scratch marks on the walls and floor. In the second, his keen eye picked out something half buried in the drifted sand in one corner — a piece of heavy twine some eighteen inches in length and tied into several knots. One end was frayed in such a way that it appeared to have been broken rather than cut from a larger piece. He studied it for a few seconds longer, slipped it into his vest pocket, and left the car.

Before he quit the area, he climbed to the top of the nearby line of dunes. Thick salt grass and stubby patches of gorse grew on the crests; the sand there was windswept to a tawny smoothness, without marks of any kind except for the imprint of Quincannon's boots as he moved along. From this vantage point, through intermittent rends in the curtain of fog, he could see the whitecapped ocean in the distance, the long beach and line of surf that edged it. The distant roar of breakers was muted by the wind's moan.

He walked for some ways, examining the surfaces. There was nothing here to indicate passage. The steep slopes that fell away on both sides were likewise smoothly scoured, barren but for occasional bits and pieces of driftwood.

Sardonically he thought: Whither thou, ghost?

21
QUINCANNON

The Meeker property was larger than it had seemed from a distance. In addition to the domino-styled home, there was a covered woodpile, a cistern, a small corral and lean-to built with its back to the wind, and on the other side of the cars, a dune-protected privy. As Quincannon drove up the lane, Barnaby Meeker came out to stand waiting on a railed and slanted walkway fronting the two center cars.

Quincannon drew the buggy to a halt abreast of him, hopped out, and joined him. The thin woman wearing a woolen cape who emerged from the car at this point seemed less impressed with Quincannon than his client was; her gaze remained cool and her mouth downturned as Meeker introduced her as his wife, Lucretia. Her handshake was as firm as a man's, her eyes animal-bright. She might have been comely in her early years, but she seemed to have pinched and soured as she aged. Her expression was that of someone who had an unhealthy fondness for persimmons.

"A detective, of all things," she said. "My husband can be foolishly impulsive at times."

"Now, Lucretia," Meeker said mildly.

"Don't deny it. What can a detective do to lay a ghost?"

"If it is some sort of ghost, nothing. If it isn't, Mr. Quincannon will find out what is behind these . . . manifestations."

"Will-o'-the-wisps, you mean."

"Do will-o'-the-wisps moan and shriek like banshees?"

"The wind did that. Plays tricks sometimes."

"It wasn't the wind. And it wasn't will-o'-the-wisps, not on a succession of foggy nights with no moon or other light of any kind."

"Your neighbor Crabb believes these sightings are genuinely supernatural," Quincannon said. "If you'll pardon the expression, the incidents have him badly spooked."

"You've seen him, then, have you?"

"I have. Unfriendly gent. He warned me away from the abandoned cars."

"Good-for-nothing, if you ask me," Mrs. Meeker said.

"Indeed? What makes you think so?"

"He's a squatter, for one thing. And he has no means of support, for another."

"According to the counterman at the coffee saloon, Crabb told Lucas Whiffing he was in construction work."

"The Whiffing boy." Her persimmon mouth puckered even more. "Sly and irresponsible, that one."

"Now, Lucretia," Meeker said, not so mildly.

"Well? Do you deny it?"

"He has never been anything but pleasant and polite to us."

"Yes, but only on Patricia's account. You know that as well as I do."

"That is of no consequence now."

"Isn't it? With him still living as close as he does?"

Quincannon asked, "Patricia is your daughter?"

"Our youngest child," Meeker said.

"Not even eighteen yet," Mrs. Meeker added. "And the Whiffing boy nearly six years older. If she'd lost her head when he came sniffing around her like a cur in heat . . ."

Her husband thumped his cane and drew himself up like a puffing toad. He said with a sharp bite in his tone, "Now that's enough.

I mean it. Mr. Quincannon's interest is in the manifestations in the cars and on the dunes, not in matters of a personal and private nature."

This was not necessarily true, but Quincannon made no comment. The Meekers were glaring at each other — a game of stare-down in which she would be victorious most times they played it. His guess proved correct when Meeker lost his puff and averted his gaze.

"Leave your horse and buggy with ours," he said to Quincannon, "and come inside where it's warm."

Quincannon did as he was bid, parking the buggy next to a Concord carriage in the lean-to. He unhitched the livery plug and turned it into the corral where a roan horse was picketed. He would deal with the animal's needs later, he decided, and returned to join Meeker and his persimmony wife.

The interior of their home was something of an assault on the eye. The end walls where the two cars were joined had been removed to create one long room, which seemed too warm after the outside chill; a potbellied stove glowed cherry red in one corner. The remaining contents were an amazing hodgepodge of heavy Victorian furniture and decorations that included numerous framed photographs and daguerreotypes, gewgaws, gimcracks, and what was surely flotsam that had been collected from along the beach — pieces of driftwood, odd-shaped bottles, glass fisherman's floats, a section of draped netting like a moldy spiderweb. The effect was more that of a junkshop display than a comfortable habitation.

Quincannon accepted the offer of a cup of tea and Mrs. Meeker went to pour it from a pot resting atop the stove. Meeker invited him to occupy a tufted red velvet chair, which he did and which was as uncomfortable as it looked. The investment broker chose to pace rather than sit, the ferrule of his stick making hollow thumps despite the carpeting on the floor of the car.

Quincannon took a sip of his tea, managed not to make a face, and put the cup down on an end table. "Now, then — these manifestations. They have all occurred late at night, I understand."

"After midnight, yes."

"When the fog is generally at its thickest."

"Yes, but not thick enough to have impaired my visibility, or my wife's, or my daughter's. Be assured of that. We saw what we saw, and no mistake."

"Will-o'-the-wisps," Mrs. Meeker said

from her perch near the stove.

Meeker cast another glare in her direction, which she returned in kind. Again he was the first to look away. "I expect you'll want to speak to my daughter," he said to Quincannon. "She should be home from school fairly soon. Hers is a rather long commute from Sisters of Bethany. I've been thinking of buying her her own carriage —"

"Unnecessary extravagance, if you ask me," his wife said.

"You weren't asked. Be quiet, can't you?"

"Oh, go dance up a rope," she said, surprising Quincannon if not her husband.

Meeker performed his puffing-toad imitation again and started to say something, but at that moment the door burst open and the wind blew in a pair of individuals, one after the other. The girl who came in first was pretty and plump, bundled inside a beaver coat and matching hat. The young man behind her, swathed in a greatcoat, scarf, gloves, and stocking cap, was none other than Lucas Whiffing. Sabina's description of him — lean, callowly handsome, blue-eyed, with a neatly oiled mustache — made that apparent even before Mrs. Meeker voiced her displeasure.

"Patricia! What's the matter with you? You know Lucas is not welcome in this home."

"Don't blame her, Mrs. Meeker," Whiffing said congenially. "I met Patricia when she arrived on the interurban and asked to accompany her."

"What on earth for?"

"I understand your guest called at my home earlier, asking to speak with me." Whiffing's gaze shifted. "You are Mr. Quincannon, the detective?"

"I am."

"Detective?" Patricia said. She had a thin, piping voice, the sort that grated on Quincannon's nerves after long exposure. "What is a detective doing here?"

"Your father hired him to investigate the silly things that have been interrupting our sleep," Mrs. Meeker said, and sniffed. "Of all the waste of money."

"Oh. The ghost, you mean?"

"Whatever it is we've seen these past two nights, yes," Meeker said.

Whiffing seemed to find the matter amusing. "A detective to lay a ghost. Are you a believer in such things, Mr. Quincannon?"

"I have an open mind on the subject. And you, Mr. Whiffing? Are *you* a believer?"

"Only in what I can see with my own eyes."

"And have you seen the alleged apparition?"

"No, I haven't."

"Well, I have," the girl said. She had shed her coat and was warming her hands in front of the stove. "Seen it and last night, heard its unearthly shrieks. It's a real ghost, Lucas. Truly. Of a man who died in one of the cars, or in a railway accident."

"Bosh," Mrs. Meeker said.

"You've seen and heard it, too, Mother."

Whiffing asked Quincannon, "Are you planning to spend the night, sir, in the hope of seeing it yourself."

"I am."

"And if you do see it, what will you do? Chase it down?"

"Whatever is necessary to find out its true nature."

"I shouldn't think ghosts can be caught."

"They can't, but fake ghosts can."

"And you believe this one is a fake? How does one go about faking spook lights and sudden disappearances? And for what purpose?"

"That remains to be seen."

Patricia said, "Mother, why don't you offer Lucas some hot tea? He must be as chilled as I am."

"If I must."

"Thank you, but I can't stay," Whiffing said. "I came only to find out what Mr.

Quincannon wants of me. Perhaps if we were to step outside, sir . . ."

Meeker said, "That won't be necessary. You may speak privately right here." He herded his wife and daughter into one of the connecting cars and shut the door behind them.

"Well, then," Whiffing said when he and Quincannon were alone. "Is it something to do with what happened to poor Virginia St. Ives that you want to speak to me about? Has her body been found?"

"Not yet. But it soon will be."

"Oh? Where do you suppose it is?"

"Where it was taken on Friday night."

"And where is that?"

"Where Mrs. Carpenter and I expect to find it."

"You know why it was taken, too, I suppose?"

"I have a very good idea."

Nothing of alarm or worry showed in Whiffing's expression. He smiled faintly, as if puzzled. Unflappable, eh? Well, Quincannon thought, we'll see about that.

"I understand you're a friend of the girl's brother, David St. Ives."

"Whoever told you that is mistaken."

"And a friend and school chum of Bob Cantwell."

Still nothing changed in Whiffing's face. "I vaguely remember Bob. But I haven't seen him in years."

"No? How long has it been since you've seen Jack Travers?"

"Who? The name isn't familiar."

"It should be. You've spent many an evening in the company of all three men at the House of Chance, the Purple Palace, and Madame Fifi's Maison of Parisian Delights, among other Tenderloin gambling and bawdy houses."

Whiffing's smile wasn't quite as fixed or puzzled now; it sagged slightly at the corners. "That is simply not true. I don't make a habit of frequenting such places."

"Their owners say you do."

"Then they are also mistaken. Really, sir, what is the point of all these remarks? Just what is it you're accusing me of?"

"Nothing at the moment," Quincannon said, "if you have nothing to hide."

"I haven't. Nothing whatsoever. Now if you don't mind, I'll be on my way." Whiffing drew the collar of his coat up over his ears and moved to the door. "Good luck with your ghost hunting, sir," he said then, and bowed slightly, and went away into the gathering darkness.

22
SABINA

Where are you, Virginia?

Sabina almost gave voice to the words, but of course it would have been a waste of breath. Wherever the girl was, she was not about to respond to a shouted demand. The only way to find her cunning hiding place was another, even more intensive search of the barn's cavernous interior.

At the Studebaker buggy, Sabina went to one knee with the lantern to peer at the undercarriage. Not there, and not beneath the spring wagon's bed, either. There were no possible places of concealment in the workroom, or in the harness room at the rear. Another climb up to the loft? No point in it, she decided. The few hay bales there hadn't been stacked, and they weren't large enough individually for Virginia to have hidden herself behind one.

That left the three horse stalls. The loose, moldering hay in two of them might be deep enough to conceal the girl, but she would have had to burrow all the way down to the bottom to avoid Sabina's surface poking. And if she'd done that, she wouldn't have been able to breathe.

Unless . . .

Sabina's memory jogged. The other lantern in the room upstairs — why was it missing its chimney? It would have smoked badly without it and was therefore useless. But the chimney alone could have another purpose, if Virginia had had the presence of mind to think of it and to snatch up the glass before fleeing down here.

A pitchfork leaned against the stanchion between two of the stalls. Sabina eyed it briefly, but decided using it might do more harm than good. She leaned into the nearest of the two deep-hayed stalls, sweeping the lantern close over the surface of the hay. Nothing caught her eye. But when she made the same sweep in the adjacent stall, the light glinted off something toward the rear. Glass. Chimney glass canted backward and all but hidden by mounded straw, which was why she'd missed it on the first search.

She set the lantern out of harm's way behind her and then reached down into the hay and caught hold of the makeshift breathing tube. "All right, young lady," she said as she yanked it free. "Come on out of there."

There was a stirring, then a sputtering cough, and Virginia St. Ives rose up out of the hay like a dusty female Lazarus. She pawed particles of straw from her mouth and eyes, glared furiously, and said three words that Sabina was surprised she knew and that might even have shocked John. Then she scrambled upright and tried to lunge free of the stall.

Sabina blocked her way, pushed her back. This served only to infuriate the girl; she launched herself forward again, fingernails slashing like talons. One of the sharp nails narrowly missed gouging a furrow in Sabina's cheek. The near miss raised her ire and she smacked Virginia across the face, as hard a slap as she'd ever administered to anyone. The blow was struck in self-defense, but the stinging pain in her hand was thoroughly satisfying. It was only a small measure of what this spoiled, destructive child deserved.

The force of the slap had driven all the fight out of the girl. She sat half sprawled against the stall's back wall, her hand pressed to her reddened cheek, her expression already defeated and sullen. "You didn't have to hit me so hard," she said.

"Oh, yes, I did. It was only a foretaste of what you'll get when I deliver you to your father."

Virginia's lower lip began to tremble. "I hate you. I hate you!"

"I don't like you very much, either, after what you've put your family and me through."

A little silence. Then, petulantly, "How did you know?"

"That you were still alive? I've known that for some time. Your primary mistake was deciding to lure me out to the overlook to witness your fake suicide, instead of following the original scheme to have it be Grace DeBrett. She would have been a much more credulous witness. But I suppose in your mind fooling a professional detective made the game even more exciting."

No response.

Sabina said, "I'll admit it was a clever trick you and your lover concocted on the cliff, but also a foolhardy and dangerous one. You're fortunate you *didn't* fall off that night, traipsing around in the dark and fog on a slippery strip of ground."

"I don't have a lover. I . . . I did it all myself."

"It's too late to try to protect him, Virginia. It took two to make the trick and the rest of your plan work. You had to have help getting away from Sutro Heights afterward without being seen and then all the way down here. While you were at the ball, Lucas Whiffing came in a borrowed or rented buggy, didn't he? And parked it somewhere outside before he slipped onto the property. Then while I was sounding the alarm, the two of you made your escape and he drove you straight down here. You must have paid a previous visit to reconnoiter, bring in the supplies you'd need, and arrange the servant's room upstairs as your hideout — doubtless the day last week you didn't return home until late." And after Lucas had dropped her off, Sabina thought but didn't bother adding, it had taken him most of the night to drive alone back to Carville. That was why he'd looked so haggard when she spoke to him Saturday morning.

Virginia offered no further denial. She said, "Lucas," in a yearning whisper. "Where is he? Is he all right?"

"For the time being."

"He was supposed to've come for me by now. He . . . oh, God." Now she looked as if she were about to burst into tears. "How did you find me?"

"It wasn't difficult, once I learned of your conversations with Arabella Kingston and paid a call on her. You had to be hiding someplace private that no one knew about while you waited for Lucas to get his hands on enough money to finance your travels. The money from the Wells, Fargo robbery. He's the one who stole it in the first place, isn't he?"

"He . . . he didn't steal it. He's not a thief."

"A thief, yes. And worse, much worse."

"I don't believe you. He's kind and gentle . . . he loves me and I love him."

"But when your father forbade you to see him, he beguiled you into faking your suicide and running off with him."

"He didn't beguile me. It was my idea. . . ."

"I don't believe you. You're not canny enough to realize your father would hire more detectives to hunt for you unless he believed you dead. He might have done that anyway, despite the suicide note, without a body to prove you were no longer alive."

Pouty silence.

"Where did you intend to go?" Sabina asked. "South? East?"

"I won't tell you."

"And what then? Live together in sin and luxury?"

"Not in sin! We were going to be married."

285

"It doesn't really matter. You're not going anywhere now except back home where you belong. And Lucas isn't going anywhere except to prison for his crimes."

Now Virginia did start to cry. Tears rolled down her straw-flecked cheeks; she made no attempt to brush them away.

"We should have left right away," she said in self-pitying tones. "That's what I wanted to do. I didn't care about the money, but Lucas said we needed it, that I'd never be happy living poor. . . ."

No, it was Lucas who would never have been happy living poor. Not that venal young man. He may have cared for Virginia, but when he knew he could never have her and access to the St. Ives family fortune by marriage, he'd wasted no time plotting his devious alternate scheme.

Sabina stepped back and picked up the lantern. "Dry your eyes," she said then, "and come out of there. I've had enough of this place and I expect you have to, if you'd admit it."

"I won't go back with you. You can't make me."

"Oh, yes, I can and will. If you give me any more trouble, I'll take you to the sheriff in Burlingame. Would you rather meet your parents quietly, like a lady, or in handcuffs like a common criminal?"

To punctuate the threat, delivered in sharp words, Sabina took the derringer from her coat pocket and pointed it in Virginia's general direction. The girl gasped, her eyes widening.

"You . . . you wouldn't dare shoot me," she murmured.

"I might, if you provoke me enough."

It was a white lie, of course, but Virginia believed it. After a few seconds she muttered something unintelligible, pushed upright, and came out of the stall. Sabina watched her warily, but there was no defiance left in the young ninny. She stood in a bedraggled slump, brushing straw from hair and clothing, avoiding eye contact. And she offered no resistance when Sabina took her arm and prodded her out of the barn, repocketing the derringer on the way.

An hour and a half must have passed, for the hired hansom was now parked on the driveway and the beaky-nosed driver was just coming down the front steps of the house. He saw Sabina with her charge and hailed her. She called back to him, asking him to wait a few minutes more, then steered Virginia to the outside staircase.

"There's nothing I want from up there," the girl said in sullen tones.

"So you say now. But we'll pack it all up nonetheless." Besides, Sabina's reticule was still in the room.

The packing took no more than five minutes. Under Sabina's watchful eye, Virginia stuffed her unpacked belongings into the two carpetbags, and the foodstuffs, eaten and uneaten, into the paper grocery sacks. The driver's eyes widened when they appeared, Virginia carrying the bags and Sabina the sacks, and he had a close look at their disheveled appearances. But he had the good sense to keep his thoughts to himself as he helped them load everything into the cab's luggage compartment.

The girl said nothing during the ride back into Burlingame. She sat slumped against one shaded window, her chin on her chest and her hands clasped tightly together in her lap. Sabina was grateful for the silence. She was tired, feeling peevish, and in need of a bath and fresh clothing, neither of which she would have for hours yet.

It was full dark by the time they reached the Southern Pacific depot. There was still time to make the evening train for San Francisco, and for Sabina to first send a telegram to Joseph St. Ives informing him that Virginia was alive and well and asking that he meet their train. She only hoped that he would receive it in time to honor her request. The sooner she was rid of the company of his duplicitous daughter, the happier she would be.

23
QUINCANNON

Alone in the parlor, Quincannon smoked his stubby briar and waited for the hands on his stemwinder to point to 11:30.

The Meekers had all retired to their respective bedrooms in the end cars sometime earlier, at his insistence; he preferred to maintain a solitary vigil. He also preferred silence to desultory and pointless conversation. There were ominous rumblings in his digestive tract as well, the result of the bland and watery chicken dish and boiled potatoes and carrots Mrs. Meeker had seen fit to serve for supper.

The car was no longer overheated, now that the fire in the stove had banked. Cooling, the stove metal made little pinging sounds that worked in counterpoint to the snicking of wind-flung sand against the car's windows and sides. As the time for action approached, he checked the loads in the Navy Colt. Not to be used against the Carville ghost, if there was such a hunk of ectoplasm; no one had ever succeeded in plugging a spook, no matter what its intentions. As a precaution, rather, because he was fairly well convinced that a human agency was behind these manifestations. He even had a notion, now, as to why, though the how of it still eluded him.

Another check of his watch showed that the time was two minutes shy of 11:30. No purpose in waiting any longer. He holstered the Navy, donned his greatcoat, cap, scarf, and gloves, and slipped out into the darkness.

Icy, fog-wet wind and blowing sand buffeted him as he came down off the walkway. The night was not quite black as tar but close to it; he could barely make out the shed and corral nearby. The distant jumble of abandoned cars was invisible except for brief rents in the wall of mist, and then discernible only as faint lumpish shapes among the dunes.

Quincannon slogged into the shelter of the lean-to. His rented plug and the two horses belonging to the Meekers, all blanketed against the cold, stirred at his passage and one nickered softly. He removed his bull's-eye lantern from beneath the seat of the buggy, lighted it, closed the shutter, then went to the side wall and probed along it until he found a gap between the boards. Another brief tear in the fog permitted him to fix the proper angle for viewing the cars. He dragged over two bales of hay, piled one atop the other, and perched on the makeshift seat. By bending forward slightly, his eyes were on a level with the gap. He settled down to wait.

He had learned patience in situations such as this by ruminating on matters of business and pleasure. Sabina occupied his mind for a time. Then he sighed and turned his thoughts to the Wells, Fargo robbery and his pursuit of the reward. The pieces of the crime and its connection to the murder of Bob Cantwell had begun to fall into place; it would not be long before he had turned up the missing ones to complete the picture. He smiled his dragon's smile in the darkness. Yes, and at the same time he might well be able to supply an explanation for the puzzling disappearance of Virginia St. Ives from the Sutro Heights parapet. It all depended on how well his hoped-for confrontation with the Carville ghost turned out. . . .

Time passed slowly. In spite of his heavy clothing the cold seeped through and his body began to cramp. A constant shifting of position helped some, though after a while it seemed as if he could hear his bones creaking and cracking every time he moved.

Midnight.

Twelve-ten.

Twelve-fifteen —

And finally there was light. A faint shimmery glow from the direction of the jumbled cars.

Quincannon strained forward, squinting closer to the gap. Gray-black for a few seconds, then the fog lifted somewhat and he spied the eerie radiance again, shifting about behind the windows in one of the cars. The longer he looked, the more distinct the glow became — and he glimpsed the shape it seemed to emanate from, the outlines of an unearthly face.

He snatched up the bull's-eye lantern, hopped off the hay bales, and went out around the corner of the lean-to. The glowing thing continued to drift around inside the car, held stationary for a few seconds, then moved again. Quincannon was still moving himself, over into the shadow of the cistern. Beyond there, flattish sand fields stretched out for thirty or forty rods on three sides; there was no cover anywhere on its expanse, no quick way to get to the cars, even by circling around, without crossing open space.

He waited for another thickening of the restive fog. When it came, he left the cistern's shadow and ran in a low crouch toward the car. He was halfway there when the radiance vanished.

Immediately he veered to his right, toward the line of dunes behind the cars. But he could not generate any speed; in the wet darkness and loose sand he felt as if he were churning heavy-legged through a dream. There were no sounds except for the wind, the distant pound of surf, the rasp of his breathing. Not until he reached the foot of the nearest dune and began to plow upward along its steep side, at which point the night erupted in a series of weird tortured moans and banshee shrieks.

A few seconds later, the wraithlike figure appeared suddenly at the crest and then bounded away in a rush of shimmery phosphorescence.

Quincannon shined the lantern in that direction, but the beam wasn't powerful enough to cut through the streaming fog. He leaned forward and with his free hand punched holes into the sand to help propel his body upward. Behind and below him, he heard a shout. A quick glance over his shoulder told him it had come from a man

stumbling awkwardly across the sand field
— Barnaby Meeker, alerted too late to be
of any assistance.

When he'd reached a point a few feet
below the crest, a wind-muffled report
reached Quincannon's ears. The ghost
shape twitched above, seemed to bound
forward another step or two, then abruptly
vanished. Two or three heartbeats later, it
reappeared farther along, twisted, and was
gone again.

Quincannon filled his right hand with the
Navy as soon as he struggled, panting, to
the dune top. When he straightened, he
thought he saw another phosphorescent
flash in the far distance. After that, there
was nothing to see but fog and darkness.

He made his way forward, playing the
lantern beam ahead of him. The grassy
surface of this dune and the next in line
showed no marks of passage. But down near
the bottom on the opposite side, the light
illuminated a faint, irregular line of tracks
that the wind was already beginning to
erase.

The light picked out something else below
as he climbed atop the third dune — the
dark figure of a man sprawled facedown in
the sand.

Gasping sounds came from behind him; a

few moments later, Barnaby Meeker hove into view and staggered up alongside. Quincannon didn't wait. He half-slid down the sand hill to the motionless figure at the bottom, anchored the lantern so that the beam shone full on the dark-clothed man, and turned him over. The staring eyes conveyed that he was beyond help. The gaping wound in his chest told that he had been shot.

Meeker came sliding down the hill, pulled up, and emitted an astonished cry when he recognized the dead man. "Young Whiffing!"

Lucas Whiffing, alias the Kid.

"What happened here, Quincannon?"

Quincannon gave no response. The victim's identity was of no surprise to him; it was only the suddenness of young Whiffing's demise that had caught him unawares, and the circumstances in which it had happened that bothered him now. Still, he might have foreseen that the situation here was volatile enough for violence to have erupted as swiftly as it had, particularly after the way he had goaded Whiffing earlier.

He cast his gaze back along the dunes. The line of irregular footprints led straight to where the dead man lay. There were no others in the vicinity except for those made by himself and Barnaby Meeker.

With a minimal amount of help from his client, Quincannon dragged and then carried Lucas Whiffing's corpse back to the lean-to, deposited it in the Meekers' spring wagon, and covered it with a tarpaulin. No purpose would have been served in allowing the body to remain where it had fallen. Meeker's daughter had a fit of hysterics when she saw the body; evidently her feelings for the deceased had been stronger than her family believed. Mrs. Meeker seemed more disturbed by this and by the prospect of a murderer on the loose in the night than the youth's death — hardly a surprise, given her feelings about Lucas Whiffing. She hurried her daughter inside the main car, where she went about lighting every lamp until all four cars were ablaze.

Meeker kept muttering, "Murdered virtually before our eyes. And by whom? Or what? It couldn't have been a . . . a malevolent spirit from the Other Side, could it?"

"Not unless ghosts have learned how to fire a handgun loaded with real bullets."

"But what I saw on the dunes . . . what *you* saw before we found poor Whiffing . . ."

"Illusion. A clever trick that backfired."

"I don't understand. . . ."

"Nor do I, yet," Quincannon said. "But it won't be long before I do."

Meeker wanted to immediately transport the youth's body to the Whiffing home, but Quincannon talked him into waiting until dawn. The dead of a fog-raddled night was no time for such a grim chore. It would be better if not easier done by daylight. There was another reason, too, that he kept to himself. The Whiffings would surely insist on summoning the city police and coroner; there being no telephones in Carville, this would require a drive into the city proper to the nearest line. The longer it took for the bloody bluecoats to arrive, the more time he would have to investigate without interference.

When Meeker had gone inside, Quincannon searched the dead lad's clothing. An old Remington single-action, top-break revolver was tucked into one deep coat pocket. He sniffed the barrel; it had been fired recently and not cleaned afterward — the weapon used in the panicked shooting of Bob Cantwell in the print shop, no doubt. And it was fully loaded; Whiffing hadn't been given a chance to use it tonight.

From the other coat pocket Quincannon fished a second item of interest: a twin of the heavy lead sinker he'd found below the parapet retaining wall on Sutro Heights. It confirmed his suspicions of a link between Virginia St. Ives's disappearance and the Carville ghost business, and gave further credence to his notion of how both mysteries had been perpetrated and why.

At dawn Quincannon helped his distraught employer hitch up the spring wagon. He had managed nearly three hours of sleep sitting in the chair before the banked fire; Meeker, red-eyed and gaunt, seemed not to have slept at all. Evidently neither had Mrs. Meeker, who came out heavily bundled and grim-visaged to join her husband on the ride to the Whiffing home. She made it plain that she was only doing so because it was her "painful duty." Patricia was "prostrated in her room, poor child," which suited Quincannon.

When the Meekers had driven away, he embarked on the morning's first order of business. As early as it was, the fog had not yet begun to recede, but the wind had died down and visibility was good. The dunes lay like a desert wasteland all around him as he trudged down the left fork at an angle between the abandoned cars and the one occupied by E. J. Crabb, who had failed to put in an appearance at any time after the ghost business began.

No smoke rose from the stovepipe jutting from the roof of Crabb's car, nor did lamplight show behind any of the windows. But Crabb was in residence. A knob-kneed horse, apparently the man's sole means of transportation, munched hay inside a makeshift pole corral nearby.

Quincannon made his way past the jumble of deserted cars, around behind the line of dunes where he'd seen the white radiance last night. A careful search of the wind-smoothed sand along their backsides turned up nothing. Opposite where he had found Lucas Whiffing was another high-topped dune; he climbed it and inspected the sparse vegetation that grew along the crest.

Ah, just as he'd suspected. Some of the grass stalks had broken ends, and a patch of gorse was gouged and mashed flat. This was where the assassin had lain to fire the fatal shot — and a marksman he was, to have been so accurate on such a foggy night.

Quincannon searched behind the dune. Here and there, in places sheltered from the wind, were footprints leading to and from the abandoned cars. Then he began to range outward in the opposite direction, zigzagging back and forth among the sand hills. Gulls wheeled overhead, shrieking, as he drew nearer to the beach. The Pacific was calmer this morning, the waves breaking more quietly over the white sand.

For more than an hour he continued his hunt. He found nothing among the dunes. The long inner sweep of the beach was littered with all manner of flotsam cast up during storms and high winds — shells, bottles, tins, pieces of driftwood large and small, birds and sea creatures alive and dead. Last night's wind had been blowing from the northeast; he ranged farther to the south, his sharp eyes scanning left and right.

Some two hundred rods from where he had emerged onto the beach, he found what he was looking for, caught and tangled around the bare limb of a tree branch.

He extricated it carefully, examined it, then tucked it inside his coat. A satisfied smile stretched the corners of his mouth as he retraced his path back along the beach and through the dunes.

The Meekers had not yet returned from their unpleasant duty. Quincannon considered the rented rig, decided it was too much trouble to hitch up. He led the plug out of the corral, slipped a halter he found in the lean-to into place, and swung up onto the horse's swayed back. The animal seemed less than pleased to be carrying so much weight, but after a few balky movements Quincannon succeeded in urging it along the dune lanes and out across the highway to the Whiffing home.

Lucretia Meeker answered his knock. Her husband had gone with a distraught James Whiffing, she told him, to summon the police and the coroner. Mrs. Whiffing was prostrate with grief in their bedroom. Lucas Whiffing's remains had been consigned to his private car to await the arrival of the coroner and the bluecoats.

"Before they come," Quincannon said, "I'll need a few minutes alone in the dead lad's car."

Mrs. Meeker narrowed her eyes at him. "What for?"

"For purposes of my investigation."

"Your investigation, indeed. If you were worth a fig as a detective you would have kept poor Lucas from being slain."

"A regrettable occurance, though there was nothing I could have done to prevent the shooting. But I won't fail in apprehending his murderer."

"That is a matter for the police, now. You are no longer employed by my husband, so don't expect to be paid for your services. He was a fool to hire you in the first place."

Quincannon had had enough of this human sourball. He stepped close, rising up on his toes so that he loomed above her like Blackbeard above a prisoner on the plank, and fixed her with a basilisk eye. "No matter what you say, I will continue my investigation until this matter has been resolved to my satisfaction. Now will you point me to Lucas's car, or would you prefer that I wake Mrs. Whiffing and trouble her for her permission?"

"You . . . you can't talk to me like that! I won't stand for it —"

"I can, I did, and you will. Well, my good woman?"

His piratical loom-and-glare withered her resistance. She muttered, "You'll pay for your rudeness, I'll see to that," but she no longer met his gaze as she showed him the way into Lucas Whiffing's private car.

He shut the door after him and turned the latch bolt. Curtains had been drawn over the windows, but enough daylight filtered in for Quincannon to see by without lighting one of the lamps. The body lay on the bed, completely covered by a blanket. The rest of the spacious room contained a stove, a few pieces of furniture, a steamer trunk, a framed photograph of contestants in a bicycle race, a poster advertising hot-air balloon rides, and little else.

Quincannon searched the dresser drawers first, then the wardrobe, but it was in the steamer trunk that he struck paydirt. Hidden underneath a layer of miscellaneous cloth items were several hand tools, a ball of twine similar to the one he'd found in the abandoned "ghost" car, a jar of oil-based paint, a board with four ten-penny nails driven through it, and half a dozen lead sinkers that matched in size, shape, and weight the other two in his possession.

Now he had proof positive of how Virginia St. Ives had "disappeared" from Sutro Heights and how spooks had been made to glow and prance and suddenly vanish in Carville-by-the-Sea.

24
QUINCANNON

Knuckles on the door of E. J. Crabb's car produced no response. Neither did a brace of shouts. But Crabb and his horse were still here, and he was up and about now: thin ribbons of smoke drifted from the stovepipe to mingle with the tendrils of fog. Quincannon used his left fist on the door, at the same time raising his call of the man's name to a tolerable bellow. This finally brought results. The door jerked open and there Crabb stood, wearing a pair of loose-fitting long johns and his dim shoebutton eyes narrowed to a glare.

"You," he said. "What do you want?"

Quincannon said bluntly, "One of your neighbors was murdered last night."

"What? Who was murdered?"

"Lucas Whiffing."

"The hell you say. Who done it?"

"From all appearances, the Carville ghost."

Crabb backed up a step, his eyes widening. "The . . . ghost? It walked again last night?"

"Same time and place as before. You didn't see it?"

"Not me. Once was enough. Ever since that time I bolt my door, shutter all the windows, and sleep with a weapon close to hand."

"That Bisley Colt of yours, eh?"

"That's right. Not that it's any of your business."

"Heard nothing, either, around midnight?"

"Just the wind. Where'd it happen?"

"On the dunes beyond the abandoned cars."

"How?"

"Shot, clean through the gizzard."

"Huh?" Crabb said. "How can a damned ghost shoot somebody?"

"A ghost didn't. A man did."

"What man? Who'd want to kill the Whiffing kid?"

"Who indeed?" Quincannon hunched his shoulders in a mock shiver. "Cold out here, Mr. Crabb. Mind if I come inside?"

". . . What for?"

"Stove warmth. And if that's brewing coffee I smell, a cup to warm my innards would

306

be welcome. You don't object to being neighborly, do you?"

"You ain't a neighbor."

"I am temporarily. Staying with the Meekers, as I told you yesterday."

Crabb hesitated a few seconds later, finally backed up to allow Quincannon to enter, and shut the door behind him. The interior of the car was meagerly furnished: a cot, a scarred table, a three-legged stool, an unpainted cabinet, a soot-blackened woodstove with a pile of driftwood beside it, and a scarred saddle and bridle for the horse outside. Clothing, dishes, utensils, and glasses, all of them unwashed and giving off a fetid scent, were strewn helter-skelter throughout. The Bisley Colt in its holster lay draped across the foot of the cot. There was nothing else of interest in sight.

Quincannon said, "Pleasant little nest you've made for yourself."

The irony was lost on Crabb. "Yeah, it's all right." He went to the stove where a tin coffeepot was heating, found a cup that was no doubt dirty, and splashed dark brown liquid into it. Quincannon made no move to take the cup from him, so Crabb set it down on the table.

"Now, then," Quincannon said. "To business."

"Business? What business? Thought you wanted the stove and coffee."

"The business of Lucas Whiffing's murder. Among other things."

"I don't know nothing about that. I told you, I spent last night locked inside this here car."

"No, you didn't, not all of it. You spent an hour or two before midnight lying in wait on one of the dunes, with that cocked Bisley in your hand."

The hard glare was back in Crabb's eyes. "What would I do that for?"

"To lay the Carville ghost once and for all."

"You don't make no sense, mister. Spook stuff scares the bejesus out of me. Ask Meeker, ask that old coot in the coffee saloon — they'll tell you."

"Spook stuff that you fear might be authentic, yes. Not the bogus kind that went on here."

"What the hell you trying to say? That I shot the Whiffing kid?"

"With malice aforethought, after you figured out he was responsible for the ghost business. And why."

"That's a damn lie! You think I'd kill some kid just because he was trying to scare me?"

"That was only part of the reason," Quincannon said. "Tell me, Crabb. What do the initials E.J. stand for?"

Crabb blinked, blinked again. "What the hell?" he said.

"The initials E.J. Your first name wouldn't happen to be Ezekial, would it?"

". . . What if it is?"

"I thought as much. Zeke for short, eh?"

"What does my name have to do with —" Crabb broke off abruptly, goggling.

Quincannon had had his right hand in his coat pocket the entire time, wrapped around the butt of the Navy he'd transferred there before knocking on the door. Now, in one swift motion, he had produced the weapon. Crabb continued to gawp, his gaze shifting back and forth between the pistol and Quincannon's face.

"Where's the money, Zeke?"

"Money? What money?"

"The money Lucas Whiffing was after. The Wells, Fargo Express money you swiped from Jack Travers after you killed him."

"You're crazy, man! Who the hell are you?"

"John Quincannon, peerless detective. Now answer my question. Where's the money?"

For a slow-witted hulk of a man, Crabb moved with the quickness of a cat. He swept the tin cup off the table, hurled it and a swirl of hot coffee at Quincannon, and lunged sideways to where the Bisley Colt lay on the cot. Quincannon managed to dodge the cup and most of the scalding spray, but the evasive action cost him any chance of putting a disabling bullet in Crabb. There was no other choice but to rush the man.

He slashed down with the Navy's barrel, striking Crabb's forearm just as the Bisley was dragged out of the holster. The blow dislodged the pistol, sent it skidding across the floor, but it also weakened his grip on his own weapon. Crabb managed to knock it into a dangle from Quincannon's index finger, nearly breaking the digit. Quincannon let the weapon drop because Crabb's arms were around him then, squeezing in an effort to snap his spine. He retaliated in kind, and they were soon locked in a grunting, gyrating contest of strength and will.

As bullish as Crabb was, Quincannon had just as much brawn and the benefit of considerable experience in this sort of hand-to-hand — or rather, arms-to-arms and chest-to-chest — roughhouse. The struggle lasted less than a minute. He ended it by dint of a mean and scurrilous trick he had learned from his father, who had previously learned it while on assignment on the

Baltimore docks, the use of which in self-defense both considered thoroughly justified. When he released his hold, Crabb obligingly collapsed to the floor unconscious.

Quincannon sleeved sweat from his brow, took a moment to catch his breath, and then gathered up both pistols. He holstered the Navy, emptied the Bisley's chambers and dropped the cartridges into his coat pocket, and tossed the useless gun onto the cot. A coil of rope was looped around the saddle's horn; he used it to bind Crabb's hands and feet. Then he commenced a careful search of the car, starting with the saddlebags.

The search proved futile. So did ones of the outside of the car, the corral, even a makeshift privy.

This served to further whet the keen edge of Quincannon's temper. He reentered the car. Crabb was still non compos mentis, but beginning to stir. Quincannon pulled the stool over next to him, straddled it, and delivered a series of none-too-gentle slaps to Crabb's cheeks until the man was awake again, glaring bloody daggers and snarling imprecations.

Quincannon drew the Navy, reached down to pull Crabb's head close, and inserted the muzzle into an unclean ear.

"Now then, Zeke. I'll ask you again. Where's the money?"

Fear glistened in the big man's eyes, but he remained defiant. "I don't know what you're talkin' about. I don't have no god-damn money."

"You're the only one who could have it. You killed two men, Travers and Whiffing, to get it and keep it."

"I never did. You can't pin no killings on me. You got no proof I shot anybody."

"Ah, but I have. That uncommon Bisley Colt of yours. Or haven't you heard of firearms identification?"

Obviously Crabb hadn't. He said, "Huh?"

"The physical matching of bullets to a particular weapon by their size and the rifling marks left on them from the weapon's barrel."

"I don't believe it. You're full of shit."

"Such crude language." Quincannon screwed the Navy's muzzle another quarter inch into Crabb's ear canal, which produced a wince and a grunt of protest. "Believe it or not, firearms identification is an established fact. Your Bisley will hang you, unless you cooperate with me as a representative of the law." It would hang him anyway, but Crabb didn't have to know that. "Well, Zeke? Are you going to cooperate?"

After a sullen half minute of silence while his small brain struggled with the decision, and another quarter-inch turn of the Navy's muzzle, Crabb concluded that he would. The defiance evaporated, and he said bitterly, "All right, you win. But I don't have the goddamn money. I never had it. You think I'd still be here if I had? Travers wouldn't tell me what he done with it."

"Then why did you shoot him?"

"I didn't have no choice. He pulled a knife on me, tried to cut my throat. I tore up the house looking for the money but it wasn't there. Thought come to me later that maybe he buried it in the yard, so next day I went back and dug around some but it wasn't there, neither."

"Did it occur to you Whiffing might have it?"

"He never went near the house after the robbery. I got that much out of Travers. Whiffing trusted him with the loot and they was gonna split when the kid was ready."

"The kid. Travers's name for him."

"Yeah. Damn fool *kid.* Travers figured to doublecross him, sure as hell. Whiffing'd be dead now anyways, saved me the trouble."

Quincannon said, "You knew Whiffing planned the robbery before you braced Travers. How?"

"He come to me with the idea first. Knew I needed money — I let that slip one of the times we talked up at the coffee saloon. He didn't have the sand to hold up the Express office himself, wanted me to do it on sixty/forty split. Said he knew when a big shipment of cash come in by train on account of the place he worked, the bicycle warehouse, was right across the street and he knew some Wells, Fargo clerk that flapped his gums when he had a few beers in him."

Whiffing's motives for turning crook were plain enough. When he realized he had no chance to marry the St. Ives girl and her family's fortune, he'd talked her into running off with him and set up the robbery for enough cash to finance the start of a new life with her. Damn fool kid, indeed. *Two* damn fool kids.

"Why did you turn the job down?"

"I figured it was too risky, wouldn't come off," Crabb said. "Otherwise why did Whiffing need me, why didn't he pull the robbery himself? Besides, I ain't no stick-up artist."

Quincannon refrained from snorting at that little slice of irony. "When it did come off, how did you know who Whiffing had gotten for the job?"

"I didn't. Said to me before, if I wouldn't do it, he'd get some other guy he gambled and whored around with who would."

"He didn't mention Travers by name?"

"No. I never knew it, never laid eyes on Travers, until the night I went up there to the house."

"How did you know it was Bob Cantwell who arranged the hideout?"

Crabb's mouth quirked derisively. "Whiffing told me. His whole damn plan, still tryin' to convince me to go in with him."

"So after you decided to hijack the money for yourself, you threatened Cantwell into telling you where Travers was hiding out."

"Yeah. Bastard must of blabbed to Whiffing, too, even after I warned him to keep his mouth shut."

Cantwell had done just that, later on, when he made the mistake of trying to blackmail Whiffing. And Whiffing had assumed, as Quincannon had, that Crabb had come away with the $35,000. The kid had not possessed enough moxie to confront a man as big and intimidating as Zeke with a drawn weapon and a demand for all or part of the swag. He might well have searched this car for the money when Crabb was away, thinking it was stashed here, but was too timid to do anything of a bolder nature. Small in stature, small in courage — a coward at heart.

Sly, half-witted tricks were his stock in trade, so he'd created the Carville ghost using the same method as in the arrangement of the St. Ives girl's bogus death leap. The idea being to prey on Crabb's fear of the supernatural — another piece of information Zeke must have let slip during their talks — until Crabb was spooked enough to take the money from its hiding place and flee with it. How Whiffing intended to get his hands on the swag at that point had died with him. Another foolish trick, perhaps, or pistol shots from ambush such as he'd done to dispose of Bob Cantwell.

A harlequinade, from start to finish, Quincannon thought disgustedly. Whiffing the court jester, and the rest of the players a bunch of buffoons. The whole dodge might have been sardonically amusing if two men weren't dead, his own head hadn't nearly been ventilated to make number three, and all the furious activity and silly game-playing hadn't been for nought. None of the dolts involved had ended up in possession of the $35,000. And the galling fact was, neither had Quincannon.

He said, "You'd better not be lying to me about the money, Zeke. It'll go twice as hard for you if I find out you know where it is."

"I ain't lying. I swear to God I ain't."

Quincannon sighed. Past experience had taught him the nuances necessary to distinguish between the welter of lies and sprinkling of truths that poured from the mouths of thieves, murderers, and other blackguards. No, dammit, Crabb was not lying.

He removed the Navy from Crabb's ear, scrubbed off a residue of earwax on the man's shirt, and once again holstered the weapon. Then he stood, put both hands in the small of his back to stretch muscles sore from Crabb's mauling, brushed grit from his coat, vest, and trousers, and started for the door.

"Hey," Crabb yelled. "You ain't just gonna leave me here like this."

"I am, for the nonce. The bluecoats should arrive in another hour or three, if not after lunchtime."

"Loosen the ropes, will you? I can't hardly feel my hands."

"No. I wouldn't want you thrashing around, hurting yourself trying to get free. Or fleeing across the dunes like the Carville ghost."

Crabb furiously suggested a physical impossibility, which Quincannon chose to ignore as he went out and closed the door behind him.

25
SABINA

Sabina was at her desk that Wednesday afternoon, writing a client's report on the St. Ives case and preparing an invoice to go with it, when John finally put in an appearance.

After she had delivered Virgina St. Ives to her angry father the night before, she had stopped by the agency before going home for her much-needed bath, food, and quiet rest. There had been no message from John then — she surmised he was still in Carville-by-the-Sea — nor any word from him since her return here this morning. Seeing him hale and hearty, if a little on the wilted side — his suit and vest needed laundering and he looked as if he had had little sleep — eased her mind.

"Ah, good, you're back from your trip," he said. He seemed to be in good spirits, but she knew him well enough to detect a tempering factor to his cheerful mood. "Did your hunch pay off?"

"It did. I found Virginia St. Ives — alive and hiding in an empty home in Burlingame." John's silent nod prompted her to add, "You don't seem surprised at the news."

"I'm not. I've known for some time she didn't fling herself off the Heights parapet. So have you, evidently."

"Yes." Sabina went on to give him an account of how she had found Virginia and the reasons the girl and Lucas Whiffing had faked her death, adding details she had omitted in her verbal report to Joseph and Margaret St. Ives. She finished by repeating Joseph's vow to deal sternly with the pair.

"He'll need only to discipline the girl," John said. "Lucas Whiffing is dead. Shot to death in Carville last night."

"By whom?"

"E. J. Crabb, the Meekers' neighbor. E for Ezekial."

"The mysterious Zeke?"

"None other. Crabb and I had a minor set-to and a long chat this morning, the result of which is that he's now in city prison on a double homicide charge."

"His other victim being Jack Travers, I take it."

"Correct."

"So then he did steal the Express money from Travers. Did you recover it?"

That was the tempering factor in John's mood; his mouth turned down at the corners. "Not yet. Crabb claims he committed his crime for naught, that he never had the money — Travers hid it somewhere and he couldn't find it."

"Do you believe him?"

"Unfortunately, yes. Crabb couldn't find it, but I will."

"Why did he shoot Whiffing? Something to do with those ghostly manifestations?"

"That, and the fact that Whiffing was the mastermind behind the Wells, Fargo holdup."

"I thought as much," Sabina said. "So our two cases were intertwined after all."

"More tightly than either of us suspected."

"What exactly happened in Carville? You solved the spook riddle as well, I'm sure."

"I did."

Before continuing, John assumed his oratorical pose. Whereas Sabina imparted information in a straightforward manner without embellishments, there was nothing her partner liked better than to take center stage, even if it was only before an audience of one, and deliver what amounted to a soliloquy. Homer Keeps had referred to him in the newspaper as self-aggrandizing; at times he could be just that, if tolerably so.

He produced his stubby briar and tobacco pouch and took his time in the loading and firing process — his favorite ploy to heighten drama. Sabina waited patiently for him to get the pipe drawing to his satisfaction and finally begin his explanations. Waited patiently, too, while he unfolded his story at length, in considerable detail and with numerous histrionic flourishes worthy of Edwin Booth. Or Lily Langtry, she thought with wry amusement. Much of what he told her she already knew or had surmised, but she didn't interrupt him.

The lengthy monologue seemed to tire him even more. When he brought his oration to a close, he sank wearily into his desk chair. But he wasn't quite done yet. He still hadn't explained precisely how Lucas Whiffing had perpetrated his tricks in Carville. Sabina prompted him by asking.

"Tomfoolery, pure and simple," he said. "The same sort he and Virginia St. Ives used to fake her death on the Heights." He paused. "The girl didn't tell you how that was done, did she?"

"No." Sabina didn't add that she hadn't needed to be told.

John puffed up a huge cloud of smoke,

rubbed his hands together, and said, "It was all quite simple, really. The central ingredient in both deceptions was the use of —"

"Kites," Sabina said.

"Kites," John said an instant later.

He blinked at her, then fluffed his beard to hide a frown. "You already spotted the gaff? How, if the girl didn't tell you?"

"A combination of observation and ratiocination, as our friend Sherlock would say."

"Bah. He's no friend of mine."

"Be that as it may, you're not the only canny member of this agency, John. I've proven that to you more than once. I suspected for some time, as I said before, that the supposed suicide leap was a sham staged for my benefit and that Virginia was still alive and in hiding somewhere outside the city. She couldn't have managed the trick alone and Lucas Whiffing was the obvious choice as her accomplice. But it wasn't until I realized the contrariety in what I witnessed that had been bothering me."

"And that was?"

"Virginia's gown."

"What about her gown?"

"I heard a distinct fluttering sound while she appeared to be standing atop the parapet, and took it in that moment to be the skirts of her gown whipping in the wind.

But in the glimpses I had just before her supposed leap, the skirts in the figure I saw *weren't* whipping about — they were motionless except for that shimmery radiance. A physical impossibility given the wind. Therefore the figure with its arms bent out couldn't have been Virginia, but rather some manufactured image of her. Once I understood that, it was a simple matter of adding the other pieces of evidence together to arrive at the truth."

"The lead sinker I found, for one."

"Yes. And the facts that Lucas Whiffing worked in a sporting goods emporium that sells kites, and was a kite flyer himself as Grace DeBrett confirmed to me. It would have been easy enough, I surmised, for a clever lad like him to build a kite made of canvas tacked onto a collapsible wooden frame —"

"Hinged in the middle, no doubt," John said, nodding.

"And fashioned in the shape of a woman and coated with an oil-based phosphorescent paint to give it substance and radiance in the fog. An experienced kite-flyer could then slip through the grounds unseen with it hidden under his coat and conceal himself beneath the parapet. When Virginia arrived at a prearranged time, he waited for her to scramble over the wall, then opened the kite and held it in place above with the aid of heavy lead sinkers — just long enough to create the illusion of Virginia standing on the parapet, when in fact she was hiding behind the fog-hidden cypress where you found the sinker.

"As soon as Lucas drew the kite down and collapsed it to hide the painted side, Virginia screamed and each of them pitched an object over the cliff to the highway below — Lucas the rock that he'd earlier set in place, to create the path through the ice plant and simulate the sound of a falling body, and Virginia the cypress limb with a duplicate of her scarf attached to it."

John's grudging but sincere admiration for her deductive skills showed plainly in his expression. The slight poutiness around his mouth, she knew, had nothing to do with the fact that she had successfully matched wits with him; unlike so many men, he harbored no ill feelings toward strong and intelligent women, else he would not have suggested their partnership in the first place. No, his self-esteem and his flare for the dramatic being what they were, it was simply that he chafed and always would chafe at having even a little of his thunder stolen, no matter whom it was who did the stealing.

To placate him, she said, "I'm sure you arrived at the same conclusions. Was it before or after you solved the riddle of the Carville ghost?"

"It was all of a deductive piece," he said. He sounded perkier now. One thing about John: even though he was prone to pomposity at times, when deflated he bounced back quickly and held no grudges. None toward her, at any rate. The ersatz Sherlock Holmes was another matter. "The only possible way in which both dodges could have been worked was with kites."

"Then you added all the clues together much as I did."

"Along with several others."

"Tell me how the spook lights were created on the dunes."

"Don't you know?"

"Not exactly. How could I? I wasn't in Carville and you were."

Further placated, John said, "The game was a variation of the one on the Heights. Whiffing knew from past conversations that Zeke Crabb was afraid of anything that smacked of the supernatural. First he told Crabb that he'd seen the lights among the abandoned cars and to watch for them himself. Then, past midnight, he slipped out, went to one of the cars, used a tool to make clawlike scratches on the walls and floor, flashed the kite he'd made — one fashioned in the image of a man and more heavily coated with phosphorescent paint — and fled with the kite before Crabb or any of the Meekers could catch him. He kept doing it, adding the banshee shrieks, when Crabb refused to be panicked into fleeing with the stolen money."

"All for naught, since Crabb never had the money."

"Yes, confound it. Whiffing was a block-head, his girlfriend no better. Their game on the Heights was a stupidly dangerous lark, as you pointed out. Whiffing's in Car-ville cost him his life."

"How was he able to run across the tops of the dunes without leaving tracks?" Sabina asked.

"He didn't. He ran along below and behind them with the kite string played out just far enough to lift the kite above the crests. To hold it at that height, he used more of the lead sinkers to weight and control it in the wind. In the fog and dark-ness, seen from a distance and manipulated by an expert, the kite gave every appearance of a ghostly figure bounding across the sand hills. And when he wanted it to disappear, he merely yanked it down out of sight, drew it in, and hid it under his coat, as he did on the Heights.

"He was about to do it again last night when Crabb, having figured out the game, lay in wait and shot him. When Crabb's bullet struck, the string loosed from Whiffing's hand and the kite was carried off by the wind. I saw flashes of phosphorescence, higher up, before it disappeared altogether. This morning I found the remains on the beach. I also found kite-making evidence in a search of his room afterward."

Sabina made the mistake of continuing to apply balm to her partner's ego by saying, "Well, I must say that was another fine piece of detecting, John."

"No finer than yours," he admitted.

"We do make a good team, don't we?"

"Indeed we do. And we could make an even better one."

"Now don't start that again. . . ."

His good humor had been restored. He actually winked as he said, "You really should give it serious consideration, my dear."

"For heaven's sake, won't you ever give up?"

"When a goal is worthwhile, John Quincannon *never* gives up."

"And when her mind is made up, Sabina Carpenter never gives in."

He smiled at her. She smiled at him.

The irresistible force and the immovable object.

26
QUINCANNON

There was a police seal on the door of the empty house in Drifter's Alley, put there after the body of Jack Travers had been removed. From the look of the yard and what Quincannon could see though cracks in the window shutters, the bluecoats hadn't done much searching of the premises. As he'd expected. Murders were common occurances in the scruffier parts of the city, and the constabulary was overworked and understaffed, as well as corrupt and generally incompetent. The discovery of an unidentified, commonly dressed man shot to death in a tumbledown back-alley house would have been given short shrift. It was only when prominent citizens were slain, or the victims were young women slaughtered by the likes of the Demon of the Belfry, or families of the deceased applied legal pressure, that the detective squad mounted a serious investigation.

The property and its environs had been deserted when Quincannon arrived, and remained so while he conducted his careful searches. The only signs of recent digging anywhere in the yard were the handful of shallow holes Zeke Crabb had created. There was nothing in the shallow space beneath the front porch except remnants of trash and a nest of spiders. Nor were there any evident burial spots among the bordering trees or in the adjacent vacant lot. If Jack Travers had planted the Wells, Fargo loot, he'd done it undetectably or in some other location.

Quincannon had no qualms about breaking into the house. He left the police seal intact and entered through by picking an unsealed lock on the rear door. If the police had added to the chaos caused by Crabb's ransacking, there was no indication of it; the interior rooms looked more or less as they had by match light on his first visit. The only apparent difference was the emptiness of the bloodstained cot in the bedroom.

He made an exhaustive search of each room, using a pry bar he'd brought with him to lift floorboards, wallboards, and wainscoting. He looked inside the stove and dismantled the flue, barely escaping a cascade of soot. He dragged the icebox away from the wall so he could check behind it. He inspected cabinets, furniture, light fixtures, ceiling rafters — every conceivable hiding place that Crabb might have overlooked.

The green-and-greasy wasn't there. Not so much as a dollar of it.

It was not in Quincannon's nature to give up on a quest, particularly one of such a remunerative nature. But what else could he do now? Only Jack Travers had known the whereabouts of the swag, and his greedy secret had died with him. It could be anywhere, close by or miles away, buried in the ground or tucked inside a hollow tree stump or an abandoned building or dozens of other places. There was simply no way to tell what sort of hiding place the crafty mind of a thief had come up with.

All the detective work Quincannon had done, all the indignities he had been subjected to — beer bath, whizzing bullets, the fight with Zeke Crabb, the unwanted helping hand from the crackbrain — and what did he have to show for it? Shared fees from Joseph St. Ives and Barnaby Meeker, yes, Sabina had reminded him of that. She might be satisfied with them, but he wasn't. Not when he could have, should have, by Godfrey was entitled to have, added so much more to the agency's coffers.

Thirty-five thousand dollars in cash — missing, lost, perhaps never to be found.

Thirty-five hundred dollars reward — gone forever.

It was enough to make even a peerless detective weep.

27
SABINA

"Sabina, dear, allow me to introduce Mr. Carson Montgomery."

Cousin Callie, in full formal regalia, with a tall, slender man in tow. Sabina, who had just arrived at the French's Victorian home, smothered a sigh. She should have known that her cousin had had an ulterior motive in insisting she attend "a small dinner party Hugh and I are giving, just a few of our more interesting acquaintances." Forever the matchmaker, that was her plump, bejeweled, and spritely cousin.

She was prepared to be her usual polite but aloof and disinterested self at such planned introductions, but when she'd had a close look at Carson Montgomery, she changed her mind. Or rather, had it changed for her. He was her age, or perhaps a few years older, and well turned out in a gray cutaway morning coat with matching trousers and a light-colored waistcoat. He had fine ascetic features and curly brown hair, but it was his eyes that held her gaze. They were a brilliant blue — exactly the shade Stephen's eyes had been. And they had the same kindly softness, but with a similar glittery light that told her he knew and responded well to danger. Eyes such as those could be understanding or harshly disapproving; loving or sparking with anger; thoughtful or suddenly gay and frivolous. In her too-brief time with her husband, she had seen just such a full range of expression in his eyes.

Callie nudged her — hard, in the small of her back. It was only then that Sabina realized she was staring, and that a warm flush had crept out of the high collar of her evening dress.

"How do you do, Mr. Montgomery?" she said, offering her hand. When he took it, his fingers felt electric on hers.

"Quite well, thank you. And you, Mrs. Carpenter?"

"Fine," she said. The one word was all she could think of.

Callie said, "Mr. Montgomery is one of *the* Montgomerys."

"Really?" Another rather lame one-word response. She couldn't seem to draw her gaze away from his.

"Yes. The Montgomery Block, you know."

"I know your name, of course," he said, "from the newspapers."

"You mustn't believe everything you read, Carson," Callie said. "The St. Ives matter was blown completely out of proportion."

"I have no doubt of that." He smiled at Sabina. "Your work must be fascinating, if sometimes hazardous."

"Yes. It is."

Callie excused herself, saying, "I'll leave you two young people to get better acquainted while I tend to my other guests." She was beaming with satisfaction as she withdrew to join her other guests gathered in the parlor.

When Carson asked Sabina if she would like some refreshment, she nodded and allowed him to take her arm and guide her to where a huge punchbowl sat on the buffet table. As he poured a cup for her, he said, "You're not the first eligible and charming lady I've been introduced to by well-meaning matchmakers such as your cousin. Debutantes, distant relatives, titled ladies, visitors from exotic foreign lands. Not to mention a woman in Modesto with three children and a grandchild on the way."

He chuckled when he said the last, and Sabina found herself responding in kind.

The fact that Carson Montgomery had a sense of humor was a point in his favor. She had never been able to abide humorless men.

"If you don't mind my saying so, Mrs. Carpenter," he went on, "none has caught my eye in quite the same way you have."

"That's a rather forward statement, Mr. Montgomery."

"But honestly given as a compliment. Do you mind?"

"I suppose not."

"I'll be even more bold. I was waiting, perhaps, for someone like you."

Stuff and nonsense, Sabina thought. Where did men come up with such pronouncements? And yet, to be fair, all men — and women — had golden words that they believed would entice, seduce, and secure. She herself had used a few upon occasion in her younger days.

"You see," he went on, "most women seem interested only in the fact that I have money and position in San Francisco society. You strike me as an exception — an independent woman with means and a mind of your own. I suspect you'd find the fact that I am also a fairly competent metallurgist who spent several years in the Mother Lode goldfields more interesting than my net worth."

She nodded, the warmth still in her cheeks. Those blue, blue eyes of his were almost mesmerizing.

While they sipped Callie's champagne punch, Carson spoke more of his experiences in the goldfields. They *were* interesting; he was an excellent raconteur. But far from the egotistical sort who spoke only about himself. He soon shifted the conversation to her and her detective work, his questions revealing a genuine curiosity and admiration for her accomplishments as a Pink Rose and as a partner in Carpenter and Quincannon, Professional Detective Services. They untied her tongue and allowed her to speak freely, to relax and completely enjoy his company.

By the time a hovering and still-beaming Callie announced that dinner was served, Sabina had permitted him to call her by her given name and had agreed to the same privilege. And when the evening ended and he asked if he could see her again, for luncheon or dinner, cocktails or a buggy ride in the park, she agreed to that, too. With enthusiasm and a stirring of excitement. He was the first man she had responded to this way since Stephen's death. Not even John had succeeded in turning her head in quite the same fashion.

John. He would be hurt when he found out, she thought on the cab ride to her flat, as he surely would if she continued to keep company with Carson. But, really, it was none of his business, was it? Her private life was her own; she had made it clear to him all along that she had no intention of mixing business with pleasure.

Then why, for heaven's sake, in spite of her attraction to Carson Montgomery, did she feel as if she were being disloyal to John?

AUTHORS' NOTE

The historical background in these pages is genuine. Adolph Sutro was mayor of San Francisco in 1895, resided on the clifftop estate called Sutro Heights, and had financed the construction of Cliff House and Sutro Baths; Carville-by-the-Sea was a budding oceanside enclave, though destined to be short-lived; the Barbary Coast and Uptown Tenderloin districts flourished as the city's lower- and upper-class seats of sin; Theo Durrant, "the Demon of the Belfry," did in fact murder and mutilate two young women whose bodies were found in the Emanuel Baptist Church in the spring of 1895, for which crimes he was hanged three years later.

It should be noted, however, that for story purposes, small but necessary liberties were taken with certain geographical and descriptive details and time elements. The world of fiction is like those that might be found in parallel or alternate universes: people, places, and events past and present are almost but not quite identical to those in the world we inhabit.

M.M. / B.P.

ABOUT THE AUTHORS

Marcia Muller is the creator of private investigator Sharon McCone and one of the key figures in the development of the contemporary female private investigator. The author of more than thirty-five novels, three in collaboration with her husband, Bill Pronzini, Marcia received the Mystery Writers of America's Grand Master Award in 2005.

Bill Pronzini, creator of the Nameless Detective, is a highly praised novelist, short-story writer, and anthologist. He received the Grand Master Award from the Mystery Writers of America in 2008, making Marcia and Bill the only living couple to share the award (the other being Margaret Millar and Ross Macdonald).